“You and [illegible] with me, in Italy. A chauffeured car will pick us up in an hour and we’ll be on my private jet and in Naples airport before you know it.”

Her mouth fell open in astonishment, then snapped shut again, this time in anger. “Oh, I see! So that’s what you were doing just now!” She hurled the words at him shakily. “Softening me up! Organizing dinner by candlelight, plenty of wine, half seducing me so I’d eagerly fall in with your plans!”

“Verity, I—”

“And then, presumably, you thought I’d not only be willing to look after Lio, but I’d be a useful little bedmate tucked away in your house! A substitute mother by day and a lover at night! How dare you?” she raged.

“It was not my intention to half seduce you.” His mouth curved wickedly, shooting her nerves into spasm. “It is not my habit to do anything by halves,” he growled sexily.

Mamma Mia!

Harlequin Presents®

ITALIAN HUSBANDS

They're tall, dark...and ready to marry!

If you love marriage-of-convenience stories that ignite into marriages of passion, then look no further. We've got the heroes you love to read about and the women who tame them.

Watch for more exciting tales of romance, Italian-style, coming soon from Harlequin Presents®!

Coming soon:

Marco's Pride
by
Jane Porter
#2375

The Sicilian Husband
by
Kate Walker
#2381

Sara Wood

THE ITALIAN'S DEMAND

ITALIAN HUSBANDS

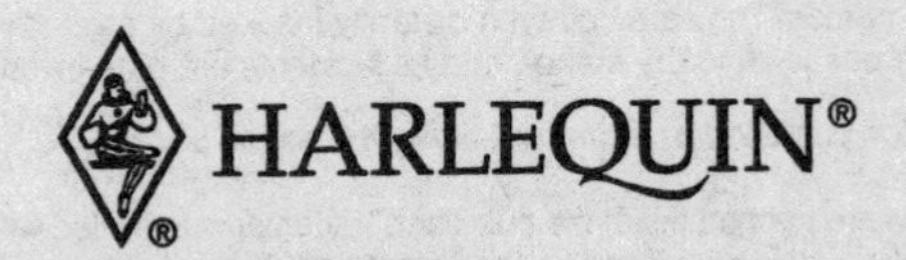

TORONTO • NEW YORK • LONDON
AMSTERDAM • PARIS • SYDNEY • HAMBURG
STOCKHOLM • ATHENS • TOKYO • MILAN • MADRID
PRAGUE • WARSAW • BUDAPEST • AUCKLAND

ISBN 0-373-12354-X

THE ITALIAN'S DEMAND

First North American Publication 2003.

This edition published by arrangement with Harlequin Books S.A.

Visit us at www.eHarlequin.com

Printed in U.S.A.

CHAPTER ONE

HE PUT down the phone and for a long time he just stared at his shaking hands, too stunned to react in any way at all. As the news began to sink in, a choking emotion rushed into the void that had been his heart.

His vision was blurred by tears of joy and he brushed them away impatiently, leaping to his feet as if propelled by rocket fuel.

Lio! he thought in amazement, racing for his study door. My *son*!

He called out, his voice cracking and husky. Then louder, till his staff came running in alarm. And then he set the house alight with orders. He requested a Mercedes to replace his unsuitable Maserati, bookings for flights and hotel accommodation and for a bag to be packed—*pronto*.

Eyes burning feverishly, Vittore hurried in long, rapid strides down the broad, sweeping steps of the *palazzo*, wrenched open the door of the car and dived in as though flames licked at his heels and the dogs of Hell were almost upon him. But he was leaving his hell behind at last.

The cream leather enfolded his lithe body. Impatiently discarding his cashmere jacket, he waited till he heard the soft 'clunk' of the boot being closed and then hastily revved up, remembering just in time a wave of gratitude to his puzzled staff.

At last. He was on his way. Expertly negotiating the tight curves of the small piazza, with the glorious Amalfi coast disappearing behind him, he eagerly headed up the hill for Naples, for London…

For his son!

He sucked in a lungful of air, barely able to contain himself. Lio, sweet Lio, was probably alive. *Alive!*

Joyous energy soared into every part of him, lengthening every muscle of his body. His breathing was all over the place: short, sharp, shallow. Every nerve danced and jerked, tuned to maximum alertness.

How could he survive the delay between now and arriving in London? How could he ever contain himself without exploding: shouting, laughing, weeping with relief…?

'Bambino mio,' he whispered softly, and the words made a vice of love and pain tighten around his heart. 'My child. My baby.'

Because soon, God willing, he would see his beloved son again, the baby he had adored with a wild and uncontrollable passion that had come upon him like a thunderclap when he'd first set eyes on his newborn child; a passion so unexpected and total that it had shaken him to his very soul and left him desperately and fatally vulnerable to all the pain that had followed.

He flung a raking hand through his neatly-groomed hair, causing a hank of it to fall, Byron-like, onto his forehead. For once he didn't care if he looked a mess, only that the love of his heart was waiting in England.

He dragged in his breath sharply, realising he'd stopped breathing. No wonder. Finding Lio again was all he'd dreamed of, night after empty night, for over a year.

He'd filled the interminable months, weeks and hours with a ferocious schedule of work to blot out the agony that had carved harsh lines in his once equable face.

The tragedy had turned him into a recluse; a cold, grim machine instead of a living, breathing man who adored life, valued friends and relatives and cared for them deeply.

But he'd had nothing to give them. No love could emerge from behind the steel cage that had surrounded his wounded heart. Life had lost its joy, its meaning.

But *now*…! Emotion suddenly overtook him again, a hard and hurting lump swelling in his throat. His son was now seventeen months old. And could soon be safely in his arms again. It would be the miracle he had prayed for in the privacy of his room, night after desperate night.

Shortly after the momentous phone call, he'd opened the nursery door which had been locked since that day fourteen months ago when his English wife Linda had abducted Lio and disappeared off the face of the earth.

Nothing had been touched. There in the middle of the cruelly peaceful room stood the beautifully carved crib in which generations of Mantezzini babies had slept and gurgled for the first few months of their lives. Above it hung the brightly coloured mobile of farm animals. In handmade wicker baskets nestled the unnaturally neat stacks of toys his son had never seen.

And the thought of his son being there again, once more filling his heart and his life with happiness and laughter, had made him sway on his feet and clutch at the door for support, taking away his very breath and robbing him of the great physical and mental strength for which he was renowned.

Darkness clouded his eyes as he remembered the reason his son would be returning. His estranged wife had died two months ago, the loan company had said on the phone.

And he, apparently was liable for the loan on her London house because she had named him as the guarantor.

He shuddered, suddenly sobered by a thought. If she hadn't forged his signature, Lio would have been lost to him forever. An ironic twist of fate.

'Poor Linda,' he murmured, offering thoughts for her salvation.

Oh, he wasn't a saint to be so forgiving of his late wife. Initially he had vilified her for depriving him of the son he loved. Yet now he felt unbelievably sad that she had died so young. Thirty years old. A tragedy.

A fear struck him. The line of his perfectly smooth jaw hardened as his white teeth jammed tightly together in an attempt to control a sharp and searing cry of visceral dread that turned his loins to water.

Dio! He didn't know that Lio *was* in the London house. He might not be. Anything could have happened to his son on Linda's death, though she'd stolen enough money to live well, to employ staff. His mother's jewels had been worth a fortune alone, and Linda had taken her own as well, plus everything in their joint bank account.

Knowing her dislike of motherhood, he assumed she would have employed an au pair or a nanny. With any luck, Lio would still be in the house under suitable care.

Unless his son had been taken away by a lover of Linda's, or some distant relative of hers. Worse, he thought, his black brows lowering in anger, the unwanted Lio could have been placed in a children's home!

He banged the steering wheel in frustration and scowled as he negotiated a tight turn in the tortuous road that snaked around the spectacular cliff.

Santo cielo! He could hardly bear it. Wanted to take chances on the slow, murderous bends, though logic curbed such rashness. It would hardly help if he were killed or seriously injured. But he longed for some means of obliterating the terrible waiting and the scouring uncertainty that was ripping his hopes to shreds.

It would be too cruel if Lio was snatched from his grasp again. He didn't deserve that.

His black eyes blazed with an intense passion. Excitement and fear created a painful chaos in his stomach and knotted his muscles even more tightly till they brought a welcome discomfort to divert his tortured mind.

Nothing, and no one must stop him this time. All his wealth, all his power, were meaningless in the face of his love for Lio.

He shuddered at the frightening intensity of his feelings, knowing that decency and caution would be thrown to the winds in his quest. The way he was feeling now, he knew he'd stop at nothing; would breach any barrier and take any steps necessary—legal or otherwise—to reclaim his beloved son.

Verity creaked her stiff body low over the sleeping child and kissed the achingly soft cheek, all the ghastliness of the past few hours forgotten in a rush of love and compassion.

What a gorgeous child. She grinned ruefully. And what a hell of a day! Amused that one had caused the other, she slowly stretched her aching limbs.

It amazed her that she felt more tired than she'd ever been in the whole of her life—even though she'd never been happier.

'Dearest Lio. Rascal.'

Her fingertips lightly touched his cute, droopingly relaxed mouth. Tenderly she smiled then lifted his sweetly dimpled arms to tuck each one, floppy and unresisting, under the sheet.

'Night, sweetheart,' she murmured lovingly. 'Little scamp, little limpet, sleep well.'

Outside the room she was forced to pause, swaying from a tide of exhaustion that rushed over her like an express train. All her energy had drained away. It felt as if she couldn't move even if her life had depended on it.

Not surprising. Her little limpet clung to her all day every day, not leaving her alone for a second. But how could she complain or push him away? It was understandable. His mother had died only two months ago. Poor Lio. Poor Linda.

Verity's expressive face folded into sorrowful lines. She thought sadly of her late, adoptive parents John and Sue Fox, who'd picked Linda and herself from the Children's Home so many years ago. She sighed. They couldn't have found two more dissimilar kiddies if they'd tried.

Life in the beautiful—and favoured—Linda's shadow had been tough. Not surprisingly, she hadn't seen her adoptive sister for ten years, their only communication being catch-up letters with their annual Christmas cards.

Nevertheless, Linda's death was tragic and Lio had suffered badly as a consequence, poor lamb.

She grimaced. So had her job, her social life and her sanity since Linda had left that note asking her to be his guardian. But she had never regretted one second of her time with Lio. The grimace became an amused smile.

It had been a moment of amazing contradictions when she'd held her orphaned nephew in her arms: joy and sheer terror had combined to confuse her. Joy because she had someone of her own at last to love. Terror because Lio wouldn't stop screaming and she knew nothing about toddlers at all.

But her mothering instincts had been awoken from that very moment and knew instantly that she would surrender everything for him. He needed her desperately—even more than she needed him, though her tender heart was still bruised from when she'd been unloved and ugly as a child and yet with vast, untapped reserves of love to give.

Lio could have every scrap of that love, she thought. And as vacant as a zombie, she dragged herself downstairs and staggered out onto the pool terrace.

Hitching up her long, floaty white sundress, Verity collapsed weakly into a welcoming sun lounger, her bones apparently non-existent amidst a mass of complaining muscle.

How could a toddler do so much damage to a grown woman? she wondered ruefully.

Her feet throbbed, her head throbbed, everything—including parts she'd never known existed—warned her not to move for hours or they'd give her hell.

She did giggle, though, when a couple of daisies fell onto her chest. Her hair must still be scattered with them after she and Lio had de-flowered the lawn and he'd solemnly stuffed every single daisy into her thick, gypsy curls. A lovely moment, she thought tenderly.

In a while, when she'd found a muscle that hadn't gone on strike, she'd have a lovely long soak in the bath. For now, she'd admire the sunset and build her strength up for the next day.

Despite a whole raft of friends, her life had been empty and meaningless. Now it was complete because of the arrival of one small baby. She sighed contentedly.

With Lio's dreadful father dead and no family to claim her nephew, it was obvious that she must adopt him. It would be only a matter of time before they were officially mother and son. She quivered with delight.

'My son,' she practised. 'Hello, I'm Verity and this is my son, Lio.'

She hugged herself. Could there be any words more wonderful than those? Could there be anything better than the slow, sweet smile of a child who adores you?

Well, perhaps it equalled a loyal, kind, tender man who smiled at her with love in his eyes and heart, she conceded. But she was all of twenty-nine and hadn't found one of those yet. Despite a huge circle of friends pushing men at her as if they were in danger of going out of fashion.

Turning her head to one side, she checked the video link with the nursery and beamed dotingly at Lio's small face.

'See you at six a.m., sweetheart,' she murmured warmly.

Soon, with the dire financial situation she faced, they wouldn't have the luxury of video links and swimming pools with palms around them, she mused. More like a cardboard box under the railway arches. If she couldn't resurrect her landscape garden business and earn some money, they'd be eating the darn daisies instead of decorating themselves with them.

'Help!' she muttered faintly. 'How can I ever work when Lio treats me like the north face of Everest and hangs on to me all day?'

Her stomach churning with worry, she hauled herself up and stood on the edge of the pool, fretfully dabbling first one bare foot and then the other in the dark turquoise water. It looked inviting, with the sunset staining the far end a glorious poppy red, but she just didn't have the energy to stay afloat, let alone swim.

On the slender cord around her waist, the entry phone buzzed intrusively. She looked at it in deep reproach. Her friends had flocked to see the incomparably beautiful Lio, vastly amused that she'd abandoned her love of freedom and independence for a child who kept supergluing himself to her.

'I'm not in,' she muttered firmly, leaving the answer button firmly switched off. It was gone nine o'clock. Too late for visitors.

The buzzing became more insistent and she silently cursed all mod cons and hi-tech appliances. Doorknockers could be ignored. Gadgets, however, had an arrogance all of their own.

'Oh, all right!' she grumbled, flicking on the switch. 'Yes? Who is it?' she demanded grumpily into the receiver.

'Vittore Mantezzini,' silked a foreign voice, declaiming the name as if it were a lyrical poem set to music.

But it was far from music to Verity's ears. It took her a moment to realise where she'd heard that name before, and then the shock made her gasp out loud.

'Vittore!' she exclaimed in horror. 'You're *dead*!'

Whirling around in dismay to face the house, she lost her balance on the wet tiles. One foot shot out sideways, her arms flailed like windmills, and before she knew it she'd gone over backwards and hit the water with a painful 'thwack' that took all the breath from her enfeebled body.

The waters closed over her head and she was in a silent world where the weakness of her attempts to surface did nothing to allay her panic. Briefly she surfaced, yelling for help, before she went down again.

The remote control for the entry phone bobbed on its cord and caught her on the temple with a sharp blow.

Lio! she thought in panic. Can't drown! He needs me!

Spurred on, she kicked strongly, feeling the sudden

warmth of the dying sun on her head, and managing to grab the side of the pool and haul herself out of the water onto her stomach, dripping, choking, gasping.

Somewhere in the distance a man was shouting. Linda's husband presumably.

'Oh, my good grief!' she groaned. *'Linda's husband!'*

Widower, she corrected, shivering with apprehension as the penny dropped. And her hand flew to her mouth to contain her appalled groan.

Of course, she thought shakily. It might be an impostor. But...if it *was* him, then somehow he'd found out about Linda's death. And that meant...

He'd come to take Lio away!

The world spun around and she clung to the ground as though she were in danger of falling off.

He couldn't take her baby, the person she most cherished in the whole, wide world, who needed her desperately and who cried piteously if she ever seemed likely to be moving more than a yard away!

Gasping for breath, she knelt up, rigid with horror. Lio screamed at strangers. He was a scared, desperately insecure little kiddie who'd been through hell and was only just learning to play.

He wasn't ready to trust anyone else. What could she do? Where did she stand in law? Would blood be the deciding factor, over and above Linda's request that he should never take charge of his child?

Verity felt sick. Vittore might be rotten all the way through, but he was Lio's father. He had a legal claim to his son.

'Hellfire!' she breathed, her mouth drying with a stupefying fear. It could be that she had no rights at all!

CHAPTER TWO

HALF-SOBBING with panic, Verity flung back her dripping hair out of her eyes and scrambled awkwardly to her feet, praying that this *was* an impostor. Perhaps someone who'd read the obituaries and thought Linda had been rich. If so, she'd tear strips off him for scaring her witless!

The buzzer made her jump. Hoping to open the gate, she grabbed the remote control that was still dangling from her waist, but it didn't work.

'I'm coming!' she yelled, her nerves perching on a knife edge.

And with her dress clinging to her like a food wrap and badly impeding her movements, she began to stumble towards the formal front garden on legs that didn't want to take her there.

If this *was* Vittore, she decided—somehow risen from the dead—then her deeply disturbed nephew must be protected at all costs, father or no father, whatever the law.

She'd run away with Lio, disappear, hide on a remote island, if it meant that his sanity was preserved.

She had a duty to the sad little baby—and was not going to hand him over to a womanising rat who'd callously ignored his son's existence—and worse.

Her teeth ground together. Vittore's infidelity had ruined the marriage and caused Linda to end her life. As a result, Lio was now an emotional mess and in no fit state to be whisked away by a strange man to a strange land where they didn't even speak English!

Rounding the side of the house, she saw him at last. Tall and immaculately dressed, he was striding up and down like a man possessed, his powerful voice ringing out as he demanded imperiously that someone come to open the high-security gate *at once*!

Vittore removed his finger from the bell, suddenly struck dumb. Coming towards him with the ferocity of a heat-seeking missile, was a tall, voluptuous woman with ink-jet hair tumbling about her head in a riot of glistening, wet curls.

And this stunning beauty was in a furious temper, a strap of her long, white dress slipping off one tanned shoulder, the neckline scooping low to the mounds of gleaming, glorious breasts which were in danger of bouncing free of the flimsy material as she careered at full speed to where he stood in silent amazement.

Awed, he drew in a sharp breath. The dress was dripping wet and draped around her body in crinkling folds so that she looked like a living Grecian goddess. Like a Venus rising from the sea.

Something kicked hard in his loins, startling and shocking him. And for a brief moment his body took control until his brain reminded him of his purpose.

'Let me in,' he ordered brusquely, short-cutting polite greetings and stamping his authority on the situation because she evidently intended to yell at him for some mad reason. He'd come for Lio, not an argument. 'I'm Vittore Mantezzini and I demand entry.'

'Oh, are you? Show me proof of identity first!' she demanded, her white teeth looking as if they would savage his flesh to shreds if he stepped out of line.

His mouth tightened at the delay and he frowned, not used to being disobeyed or challenged. Slid a hand into the inside pocket of his cashmere jacket and handed over his ID card without further comment.

Though the angry set of his jaw and the black glitter of his hard, cold eyes would have deterred most people from questioning his word.

Scowling, she peered at the photo, then checked that it

looked like him. Since it had cost a great deal of money and the efforts of Milan's top society photographer, there was, indeed, a flattering likeness.

Shock registered on her face. Then undisguised dismay.

'You're dead!' she protested, searching his narrowed eyes in bewilderment, her soft lips parted in a perfect O.

Touch me, find out how alive I am! he almost said to his own astonishment, but stopped himself in time, a curl of heat lazily nevertheless easing his tense muscles.

It was new, this. To live again, to breathe sweet air, to feel emotion and the lure of an attractive woman…

'Is that what Linda told you?' he queried, annoyed at being diverted by a pretty face, even for a second. Pretty? No, beautiful. Unique, he corrected before he could help himself. Amazing what happened, he thought, when joy captured your emotions.

Plainly crestfallen that he wasn't six feet under, she nodded unhappily. 'Last summer,' she replied in a hoarse whisper. To his astonishment, he noticed that her hands were trembling. She swallowed, the slender line of her throat oddly vulnerable as she did so. 'Linda sent a change of address,' she continued. 'That's when she said you were dead and that she had come back to England with Lio.'

'Linda was lying,' he said curtly. 'I'm very much alive. As you see.'

She stared at him hard, as if reassuring herself that he was, indeed, not a mirage. Beneath her solemn gaze, he drew himself up and stared back. Apparently she detected enough life to convince her because she gave a little shudder, almost a sexual response. Her shoulders fell in disappointment. He wondered why and was about to ask when she spoke again.

'If I'd known you weren't dead,' she mumbled, her voice wobbling in distress, 'I would have contacted you when… Oh!…' Her hands flew to cover her mouth in alarm. 'You know,' she said, somewhat inaudibly, 'that Linda herself is—?'

'Dead. Yes.' He brushed her apology and her tact aside with an impatient gesture. She looked shocked at his dismissal of his late wife's death but the past was past, the present full of urgency. 'I want to see my son. Now,' he announced irritably.

'Tough!'

He almost reeled back in shock. Something odd was happening here. 'What did you say?' he asked menacingly.

'It's impossible!'

With her extraordinary violet eyes flashing in challenge, she flung back her head, releasing a shower of water drops from her dripping hair. Intrigued, he noticed that tiny white flowers had been trapped in the tar-slick curls. Daisies. Very bohemian.

Her hands thumped belligerently down to her hips, drawing his gaze there. Incomparable, he thought with a start, his eyes and brain full of delicious curves. In other circumstances it would have been the body of his dreams. But he had something more important on his mind.

'Because?' he growled, eyes glittering with shards of white-hot fury.

She glared, as hostile as if he were the devil incarnate. 'Because you can't! Because I'm not going to let you!'

He froze, fearing that she'd say his son had disappeared. Drawing in a steadying breath he jerked out a husky, 'And why the hell not?'

'Because he's asleep!' she declared, defiant and ready for a pitched battle.

But her words were wonderful. The best news he could have had. Vittore's eyes closed and his heart lurched wildly, every taut muscle unwinding as if by magic.

Lio was there! Thank you. Thank you, he thought fervently.

For a moment he couldn't speak for emotion, but he knew he must persuade this ill-tempered vision to open the gate before she turned out to be a figment of his fevered imagination.

'It doesn't matter if he's asleep or awake,' he said shakily, his heart singing for joy. 'I just want to see him. He's my son!' he cried passionately. 'You can't stop me. So open the gate at once!'

The curving red lips were bitten, one then the other, by the small, white teeth. Her face was a picture of misery, her entire body slumping in defeat and she shivered pathetically.

'No. I've got to get dry,' she mumbled, her eyes tragic. 'I'm absolutely soaked—'

'I'd noticed,' he drawled. He wasn't blind. His iced-over sexual responses had already made themselves known, much to his surprise. 'Are you all right?' he enquired, his innate thoughtfulness temporarily overriding his own agenda. 'I heard a cry—'

'That was me. I was startled to hear your name because you were dead. Or so I'd thought. I fell in the pool,' she explained mournfully. 'Swimming in a long dress when you're exhausted isn't the easiest activity in the world.'

There was a breathless silence while he followed her rueful glance at the dress, which seemed to have become an intimate part of her body. Every mound looked alluringly attainable.

Overcome, he pushed a hand over his forehead as his head swam with tiredness from travel, from expectation—or were those the stirrings of sexual desire?

Ruthlessly he restored some semblance of control. 'I'll take your word for it. I've never tried. So it's my fault you're wet?' he queried, sounding more sardonic than he had intended.

She glared, piercing him with her pansy eyes, thick black lashes wet and spangled with tiny drops of water. He couldn't stop the heat coursing through his veins. *Maledizione!* He felt shaken by her, as if he'd been hit by a truck. But of course, she was so vibrant, so alive, and his emotions were at fever pitch…

'It certainly is!' she retorted sharply. 'So you'll have to stay here while I go and change—'

'*Dio!* What are you trying to do to me?' he cried in astonishment. The thought of waiting a second longer had effectively reined in his wayward hormones. 'This is ridiculous! Let me in now!' he ordered indignantly.

'No. You wait!' she repeated in agitation.

'The devil I will!' he raged. 'Surely you don't intend to keep me hanging around out here, prowling up and down like a caged tiger, while you—'

'I *have* to!' she cried, clearly agitated. 'I can't risk you snatching Lio while I'm changing!' she flung.

Vittore flinched with horror at such a barbaric idea. 'Snatch? Why should I snatch what is mine?' he demanded in outrage.

'*Yours?* Oh, help!' she muttered. 'Where do I begin? I'm just protecting Lio—'

'From his own father?' he asked incredulously.

'Yes!' Her hand swept impatiently over her forehead. 'Look—you must wait. I promise I'll let you in as soon as I can. I'm a quick dresser. I just can't risk...' She fidgeted in agitation, artistic fingers twisting and writhing together. 'There's something you have to know—'

'What? Why?' he grated in helpless fury. 'And what right do you have to deny me? Just who the devil are you?'

'I'm Verity,' she replied wearily. 'Verity Fox. I was adopted by the Foxes, like Linda. I'm Lio's guardian. Stay there. Won't be a sec.'

With that, she spun around, untwisted her skirts impatiently and gathered them up to reveal long, tanned and bare legs, which suddenly leapt into action and took her around the back of the house again in a flash of shimmering gold and white, all topped off by that night-dark, bobbing hair.

He dragged his mind from this vision, realising he was being left to stew.

'Come back!' he shouted angrily. 'Verity! Come back at *once*—!'

He was talking to thin air. He felt like bellowing in his frustration. A nanny or au pair would have been easier to deal with than this stunning, feisty woman with a knock-out body and a mind of her own!

He pressed a hand to his forehead, feeling as if he'd been standing in the path of a hurricane. He thrummed with life, aroused by Verity's extraordinary persona, fired too by the tantalising knowledge that his son slept peacefully a hundred metres or so away.

Patience, he told himself, trying to calm his agitated mind. Five minutes, ten, an hour…what did those minutes matter in the long run? Lio was in the house. He'd scoop him up in his arms and never let him go. Soon. *Soon.*

But logic and sense couldn't compete with months of deprivation. He wanted his child and had been without him too long.

'For the love of heaven!' he groaned contrarily.

How *could* he wait? How long did it take most women to undress, shower, choose something suitable… Hell. Hours, usually.

Suddenly incapable of remaining still, he began to loose off some of the energy that seemed to be stored in his body by striding up and down. Astonishingly, his mind had leapt away from Lio and had focussed on the woman who'd ignited his consciousness, imagining her in a room upstairs, peeling off that dress…

Per l'amor del cielo! What was he? Some sort of sex maniac that he should be distracted by a fabulous body at a time like this? It was true she was beautiful. Luscious. Perfect skin, incredible eyes, a mouth that had been made for kissing. And she was fiery. Passionate and apparently very caring.

He allowed himself a wry smile. No wonder she'd made such an impression on him! It was because his feelings were all over the place, his needs raw and hungry. He'd be more in control once he'd seen Lio. More tranquil.

'Avanti!' He muttered impatiently. Come on!

He had a child to hold and love, bags to pack, a flight to catch. A son to take home.

From the upstairs bedroom, the trembling Verity furtively observed Vittore as he fumed his way up and down beside the burglar-proof railings. Once he stopped and looked up at the spikes at the top and seemed to contemplate climbing over, but he then thought better of it and resumed his furious prowling, for all the world like the caged tiger he'd mentioned.

She gulped, her eyes wide with dismay. Never in the whole of her life had she seen anyone so angry. He simmered like a rumbling volcano about to erupt and devastate the countryside around.

Her heart thudded loudly. Vittore wouldn't meekly go away when she explained that Lio oughtn't to leave her. He'd never understand. She knew that he didn't have an ounce of sensitivity in the whole of his body.

The nausea clawed at her stomach again. It looked horribly likely that she'd lose Lio. This was a situation she hadn't expected, not in a million years.

She would never have given her heart so completely if she'd thought Vittore might turn up. Wouldn't have allowed Lio to regard her as the centre of the universe. It would devastate her if Lio left. And how would he ever recover?

'Oh, God!' she whispered, appalled by the terrible dilemma.

This was Vittore's child. But Lio was far too disturbed to be put in his father's care. Verity held her stomach, willing herself not to be sick. She had to get through this, had to succeed, for Lio's sake.

Her brain whirled with questions. Linda had lied when she'd said that Vittore was dead. Why? Had she run away?

And if so, why? What kind of ogre was Vittore? Or was it his persistent infidelity that had been too painful to bear? Linda had been scathing about his womanising.

Verity took a good, hard look at him. Not that she didn't know already how sensual he was, the kind of man who'd attract women like flies to his web.

That athletic and muscular body was packed with sexual impulses—which had, she could have sworn, been zapped at her once or twice. She'd certainly found herself reluctantly wilting under the intensity of his hot, sultry eyes. He even moved with a sexy fluidity that had made her knees go weak.

His air of sophisticated, man-of-the-world confidence was very appealing. Vittore's hair was glossy; smooth and neat, now he'd swept back that poet's lick back from his forehead. And he probably made good use of those melting chocolate eyes that had expressed several emotions in the short time they'd talked; flashing with tenderness, anger and longing.

She groaned in despair. It seemed that he wanted his child badly. Whether that was just a male need for a son and heir, or for a more profound and worthy reason, she didn't know.

Linda's boasts about their lifestyle could have been true. Clearly he was rich and successful, which meant he was used to getting whatever he wanted. She knew he headed the family textile business, with masses of exclusive outlets all over the world. So we're talking about dynasties, she mused gloomily.

Even if she hadn't seen the Mantezzini name above adverts for impossibly glamorous and expensive clothes, she could have recognised his wealth in the cut of his quiet, classy, soft-textured suit. It fitted him like a glove and had obviously been hand-made. Shoes, too. Probably the cream shirt and expensive silk tie had been laboured over with loving care as well. Yes, the playboy Italian looked groomed to the last immaculate inch.

Smelling of money. Smelling gorgeous, as a matter of fact, drat him! She scowled. He'd give Lio a fabulous life—far better in material terms than the one she'd envisaged for them. No doubt Lio would take over the business eventually. What a future.

But would her nephew have what truly mattered: total, unconditional love? She went cold, envisaging the kind of loveless existence she'd been subjected to at home. Without her friends at school, she would have been utterly miserable.

And who would offer Lio a mother's love? Would he find an ever-changing string of women in his father's bed? And...would he be farmed out to nannies and be visited by his father only at teatime?

Her fists clenched. That wouldn't be good enough! Bewildered, frightened little Lio needed affection and love like a fish needs water. And he needed Vittore's rotten kind of fathering like a hole in the head.

But...what was she going to do? Start a siege? And look what a bag of nerves she was! She was trembling all over!

Time she dived into a warm shower. And found the courage to persuade Vittore that he couldn't take Lio away right now.

She dared not fail. Her stomach lurching uncomfortably, she checked that Lio was all right. Looking down on his sweet face, her heart somersaulted at the thought of the next hour or so which would decide his fate as well as hers. Her finger stroked his fair cheek.

'Oh, Lio,' she whispered brokenly. 'I love you so very much!'

A sob escaped in a wobbly kind of sound through her trembling lips and she hurried to peel off her sopping wet dress. Shakily she stepped into the shower, where tears mingled with the water that poured over her head and where all the daisy petals from that lovely, blissful afternoon were swept away, to sit in a limp and miserable heap blocking the shower drain.

Still only half-dry, her hair wrapped in a virgin white towel, she wriggled into the first pair of briefs that came to hand and yanked what she thought was her cotton turquoise dress from the wardrobe, her fingers shaking so much she could hardly cope with the tiny buttons which ran from neckline to hem.

Too late, she discovered it was a similar one of Linda's: too late, too short and too tight, she thought moodily, diving for the buttons in order to take it off again. Just then, the gate buzzer rang shrill and loud, and she jumped, fearing that Lio would wake.

'Damn whoever forgot to make you waterproof!' she muttered, glaring at the ruined entry phone remote control which she'd flung on the bed. 'Where were you when I needed you?' she demanded.

The wretched thing might have let Vittore in without any further risk of awakening the sleeping Lio. As it was, Vittore had apparently decided to lean on the buzzer till she answered and it was screaming through the silence of the house like a banshee.

And so, barefoot and muttering all the rude words she knew, she hitched up the pelmet skirt to hip level and hurtled down the stairs to punch in the code that opened the gates. Remembering, of course, to snuggle the skirt back as far as it would go—which wasn't far. Not that she cared.

All she could think of was that Vittore could destroy her happiness and turn a bewildered, distressed child into a total wreck. Her heart leapt erratically, her mind focussed only on Lio. His interests came above everything else.

Wiping her clammy hands on her hips, she opened the front door and drew in a horribly shaky breath as the scowling threat to Lio's welfare came up the drive and strode grimly up the wide steps towards her, his intention crystal clear.

He'd demand to see Lio. Order baby things to be packed. *And there wouldn't be a thing she could do to stop him.*

CHAPTER THREE

'COME IN,' she whimpered in an appallingly silly, breathless voice.

Vittore obviously thought she was ditzy because he frowned.

'Lio,' he stated starkly, not beating about the bush.

'You mustn't wake him!' she declared tremulously.

The rich chocolate eyes hardened. 'Sweet Madonna—!' He checked himself, his sultry mouth a thin, angry line. 'Just point me in his direction. Upstairs, is he?'

Seething with anger, Vittore started striding towards the opulently grand staircase and she had to scurry frantically to catch him up, the towel falling off her hair in the process.

With water dropping onto her bare shoulders, she reached out and grabbed his arm. He stopped dead, gazing at her inscrutably.

It was like gripping tensile steel. Alarmed by the illogical intimacy of what she was doing, Verity snatched her hand away. Tingles were whizzing up and down her arm. The man was electric, she thought in confusion. And, heaven help her, she'd just been switched on.

'Yes?' he growled, in a deeply husky voice that somehow made her knees turn to water.

She swallowed, some crazily diverted part of her brain mulling over the fact that he seemed to extend words, savouring them in his mouth and letting them roll out in an unnervingly sexy way. That was Italians for you.

'You've got to promise,' she breathed, astonishingly still not in full control of her lungs. Or anything else for that matter. Fear did funny things to the body.

'Promise what?'

Valiantly she pulled the wandering strands of her brain together and licked her dry lips till she could speak again.

'Promise not to wake him!' she croaked.

'So. You care about my son,' he observed, scrutinising her anxious face as if interested in every detail.

'*Yes!* I adore him, every little scrap of him!' she cried, all the passion in her heart filling that declaration with a fierce intensity. 'From his little toes to the top of his blond head!'

For a moment his watchful eyes seemed to soften. She did, too. He was mesmeric. She couldn't tear her gaze from his.

'I won't wake him,' he promised, solemnly gazing deep into her eyes. 'Just…' It seemed that emotion had got the better of him. For a second or two she watched wide-eyed while he steadied himself again. 'You will understand,' he said softly, 'that naturally I am anxious to see him after all this time.'

'But not *take* him!' she faltered.

'That, Verity, is why I'm here,' he pointed out drily.

She felt faint. 'You mean you're just going to pick him up out of his bed and shove him in your car and drive away?' she cried in horror.

Vittore flinched. 'Do I look like a barbarian?' he asked coldly.

'I don't know what barbarians look like, do I? I have to protect him!' she jerked in distress. 'I am his guardian!'

His brows dipped together alarmingly and she realised she'd insulted him unforgivably by suggesting he was an uncouth savage.

'Is this a legal guardianship? An official arrangement with signed agreements, ratified by a solicitor?' he shot at her unfairly.

She shuffled her feet, unable to lie but wishing she could.

'N-no—'

'Then you have no right in law where he is concerned,' he said, crushing any hopes she might have harboured.

'Law! What does the law matter—?' she began hotly.

'Everything!' he barked. 'Now listen, Verity. I've had enough of your hostility and suspicion. I suppose you've had Linda's version of events. Well, this is mine—'

'I know all about you!' she yelled.

'No, you don't! You've heard nothing but lies. You will listen if I have to tie you up and gag you first!' he raged.

She cringed back, frightened by his raw anger. She might have to call the police if he got violent. But her best bet would be to humour him, let him see Lio and then give him the facts.

'I'm listening,' she said coldly. 'Go ahead.'

He folded his arms, his eyes dark and brooding and she realised that the bleakness of his expression was actually nothing to do with her, but some pain he'd held within him for a long time. Something in her suddenly sympathetic expression must have soothed him, because he gave a helpless gesture with his hands and muttered a curt, 'Thank you.'

Then he fixed her with his penetrating eyes and began.

'Fourteen months ago, Linda abducted Lio from my house,' he said stiltedly. 'I had no warning. When I left for work, he was there. When I came home, he and his mother had gone. Linda's dressing room was empty and all of Lio's clothes had been taken away. I heard nothing. Knew nothing. My son had vanished off the face of the earth. For all that time, I didn't know if he was dead or alive. Until this morning—'

Verity felt his pain, her stomach constricting with horror. 'I can't believe this!' she gasped. 'You thought he might be dead? That's *terrible*! How could you bear it? If what you say is true—'

'*True?* Of course it's true!' he exploded. 'Why would I pretend otherwise?' he fumed. 'Do you think I *enjoy* tormenting myself with the memory of the suffering I endured at the hands of your adoptive sister?'

She flushed. 'I don't know! I have two conflicting stories and I'm confused! It's just that it was such an extraordinarily cruel thing to do, and…'

'It was,' he rasped. 'How else could Linda deal me a mortal wound?'

'Oh!' Verity breathed, wide-eyed with shock. What had happened between him and Linda, she wondered? 'She must have hated you very much!'

Pain etched lines around his eyes and mouth. 'I'm not discussing her any further,' he said tightly.

She knew when not to probe. There were terrible undercurrents here she knew nothing about. To do something so drastic, Linda must have been provoked beyond endurance!

Verity's eyes grew even larger with apprehension. She leaned against the banister, clutching at it for support, even more determined not to hand her precious, needy Lio over to this deeply flawed man.

'I didn't have the full story, obviously.' Her chin lifted in a stubborn gesture, huge violet eyes flashing in warning. She vowed that she'd get to the bottom of this before she let Vittore touch a hair of Lio's head! 'I don't think I have it *now*—'

'Verity,' he muttered tautly, barely controlling his temper, 'I am trying to remember my manners, but I am becoming increasingly impatient. Control comes easily to me—except where my passions are fiercely engaged. As they are now. For the last time—are you going to show me where Lio is, or do I search for him myself?'

'I'm afraid you'll take him away!' she jerked.

'Of *course* I will!' he flared. 'He is my flesh of my flesh, bone of my bone! Sweet heaven, I have held him in my heart and ached for him every hour of every day since he was taken from me!'

His words rang true and touched a chord in her. He

wanted his son. Had a right to him. Her head bowed in defeat and drops of water fell from her swinging hair, staining the front of her dress. The painful thought of losing Lio felt like a dozen daggers in her breast. Imagining little Lio's anguish only added to her pain.

'Oh, no!' she groaned. 'No...'

As her despairing body wilted and it seemed she'd fall, strong hands caught her arms, holding her up as if she were weightless. Dizziness claimed her but she knew she had to stay alert and desperately struggled to focus her mind.

'Verity!' he muttered urgently. 'Whatever is the matter?'

'Terror!' she blurted out tearfully.

'What?' His perplexed face was close to hers, a blur of golden skin and strong, white teeth. 'Explain!' he demanded.

Tipping up her plaintive face to his, she tried not to drown in the dark liquid eyes.

'I'm t-terrified you'll walk off with him *now*. He's only a baby, Vittore and he'll be so frightened if you do!' she cried tremulously. 'Don't take him till I've talked to you!' she begged in one last, desperate attempt. 'Please, Vittore! For Lio's sake, you need to know everything about him!'

He looked wary, his eyes narrow and glinting with troubled lights as they searched hers.

'What do you mean? Is he ill? Physically harmed?' he fired harshly, startling her.

'No! He's physically perfect.' She winced at the pressure of his hands. 'Please! You're hurting me!'

'Forgive me!' His body, his grip, relaxed. 'I do apologise. I was upset. Worried. In my anxiety I didn't realise what I was doing.'

Gently he rubbed her arms where his fingers had clamped so tightly but she could see that his thoughts were elsewhere.

And she was glad, because she had shuddered at his touch. The strain of the moment was making her supersensitive—just when she wanted to be cool and composed.

'You unnerved me,' he said shortly. 'For a moment, I feared the worst.'

'Please don't worry. He's gorgeous,' she assured him. 'But… Look. Go and see him. Then let me talk to you!' she begged.

He frowned, then shrugged. 'All right. Anything. We'll talk. *Briefly.* I have a flight booked.'

Verity suppressed a moan. A flight! Not with Lio in tow, she vowed. She'd make sure of that. But at least he'd agreed to listen to her. She had the chance to persuade him that whisking his son off to Italy would be a terrible mistake.

'Thank you!' she whispered.

To her dismay she felt her legs buckle. Vittore drew her close again. For a moment she let her head rest against his solid chest, glorying in the protection of his embrace. Men had held her before, but only because they wanted to kiss her. No one had ever wrapped her in their arms and soothed her with stroking fingers, as Vittore was doing now.

Not even her adoptive mother.

Being cherished—however briefly—was a wonderful revelation. She could get addicted to it. But she knew she had to pull away.

'I'm a fool. Sorry to be so feeble,' she mumbled, not daring to meet his eyes. Embarrassed, she pushed back her hair and said jerkily, 'And now I've made your shirt wet.'

'It'll dry.'

'I'm usually strong and positive,' she hastened to explain, absently taking his handkerchief from his top pocket and dabbing at the shirt aimlessly. Till she felt the warmth of his chest beneath, the strongly beating heart beneath her resting fingers. And stopped suddenly. Tucking the hanky back, her face scarlet with confusion, she added without thinking, 'But…I'm so worried about Lio!'

Vittore's eyes narrowed in shock. 'Why?'

Oh, help! she thought, with a silent groan at her stupidity. She'd meant to tell him in a calm and rational way so that he realised she wasn't making a drama out of nothing.

'I don't know where to start. It's a long story—' she began hesitantly.

'*Cielo!* All these hints, these warnings... Where is he? Show me at once!' he ordered grimly, on the edge of another explosion.

Somehow she pulled herself together. Squeezed enough air into her lungs to whisper a 'follow me', and to get her up the stairs. Guided him to the open nursery door.

'There,' she said shakily.

'Thank you,' he grunted.

He inclined his head with a sharp jerk to accompany his thanks but didn't immediately go in. Wide-eyed and distressed, she stared while he stood as still as a statue, the slight shaking of his hand on the door jamb the only indication that he was under considerable strain. And then, squaring his shoulders, he walked into the half-darkened room.

Shaking like a leaf, Verity watched from the doorway. And her entire body weakened as he slowly moved forwards, his eyes intent on the sleeping Lio, every line of Vittore's body revealing how deeply he must have yearned for this very moment.

'Lio!' he whispered on a zephyr breath. His lips parted, his rapt face showing the bitter-sweetness of anguish and joy. '*Piccolino,*' he murmured tenderly. 'My little one. *Ecco Papa! Daverro*...you are so *beautiful*!'

Tentatively he reached out and touched the side of the cot as if it were made of beaten gold. She could see that he was studying Lio with the kind of detailed attention that only a doting relative would display.

Her heartbeats thundered in her ears. She knew what he was doing. Many a night she'd done the same—and for him, this was the first time he'd seen his son since...her forehead wrinkled in deep thought. Since Lio was about three months old, she estimated. How awful! What a nightmare he'd suffered.

Yes. She'd been right. Every hair of Lio's gorgeous white-blond head was being meticulously recorded and mentally stored as if Vittore feared his son might be snatched from his grasp again and he'd have to rely on memory alone.

Now the bold sweep of the baby's brow and the honey-gold skin which was so flawless and kissable. The heavily lashed eyes—black lashes, extraordinarily, probably inherited from Vittore. That dear little mouth, button nose and stubborn chin—oh, so horribly stubborn!

One dimpled hand had flung itself on the wafer-thin pillow in abandon, the fingers curled loosely. She saw Vittore eyeing it fondly, longingly, swallowing as he pushed back his emotions.

Her eyes filled with tears and hot prickles of heat came with them. He would love Lio. How could he do otherwise? It was a wonderful moment, she told herself. A father bonding with his son.

But a nasty little voice inside her scuttled around, wishing that Vittore hadn't given a damn, had never come, never been enchanted by the most beautiful baby in the whole wide world.

Because Lio mustn't be parted from her. Not for a long time. His emotions were too fragile. He needed stability and reassurance, not strangers, strange surroundings, the confusion of the incomprehensible words of another language.

So...what was she to do?

Quietly Vittore sank to his knees and reached out, very delicately, to the half-curled fist. Lio's fingers instinctively closed around Vittore's hand and he let out a jerk of breath as if that small and relatively insignificant action had seared his heart and branded him forever as a worshipper at Lio's feet.

It all but broke her heart, too. Watching Vittore so

openly adoring his son was one of the most touching and painful things she'd ever witnessed. And she couldn't bear to stay any longer.

Out on the landing, she mopped at her tears and tried to organise her wayward lungs again so that she wasn't having to deal with the huge, irregular sobs that hurtled up into her throat and leapt out, taking her unawares.

'He's...more beautiful...than I remember. Has grown... so much...'

Vittore's strangled sentence and mangled words suggested that he, too, had almost lost the power of speech. Knowing she'd crack up if she looked at him, she nodded and gave a quick jerk of her head to invite him downstairs.

They went down very slowly, in total silence. But she felt overpowered by his tension. It clawed at the air, suffocating her with its electrical charge, crushing what little energy she had left. She wanted to howl.

'Drink?' she croaked, when they had fetched up in the drawing room.

'Whisky,' he husked back. And then barely recognisable came, 'Thanks.'

Hardly able to stand, she poured two stiff measures, spilling some on the tray. And felt she could down both drinks. Without a word, without meeting his eyes, she handed him the glass. Her hand was shaking. To her amazement, so was his.

Startled, she looked up and felt every part of her body go into meltdown. She'd never seen a man looking radiant before. It was...utterly irresistible, his smile just heart-wrenchingly blissful. Her head seemed to spin.

He loved Lio desperately. Wanted him more than ever. She felt terrible. This would be so painful.

'Please. Sit down,' she whispered.

And took a huge gulp of her drink. At the moment he was in Paradise. She'd ruin that for him. He wasn't going to like this. Her legs shook. He was powerful. Dominant. A man of power. He wouldn't take kindly to being thwarted. And he might ride rough-shod over her argument, dismissing her pleas and going his own sweet way.

Liquid slopped over her fingers. She dumped her glass on a small table before it slipped from her boneless fingers.

Dear heaven. She must convince him. Where to start?

In his own happy world, clearly deeply content with life, Vittore folded himself elegantly into the opulent sofa and crossed one long leg over the other.

'I presume it's you who has been looking after Lio,' he murmured. She nodded, not trusting herself to speak. He produced a dazzling smile, fed by the rapture in his heart. 'I am eternally grateful to you,' he said softly, his pleasure all the more poignant because she would be the one who would dash his hopes and turn that smile to tight-lipped fury. 'You can be assured that I will show my gratitude with a generosity that—'

'No! I don't want money! I don't want your gratitude!' she cried frantically, her nerves jangling too much for any polite, considered response.

She jerked up her head angrily, staring at him in desperation. Just let me have Lio, she thought hopelessly, knowing that was impossible and wrong, but wanting it just the same.

He shrugged elegantly, his hands palm up in an eloquent gesture. 'You have my gratitude, whether you want it or not.'

She realised how much he used his hands, how they graphically emphasised his anger, determination and love.

When he'd spoken of Lio, his movements had been gentle and caressing. When he'd soothed her just now, they'd moved sympathetically and with infinite tenderness…

A flurry of heat moved lazily through her body. She was stunned to recognise it as sexual desire. Verity bit her lip, aware she was in danger of becoming dazzled by the handsome, charismatic Vittore. He'd twist her around his little finger if she wasn't careful, and she'd find herself waving goodbye to a shrieking Lio before she knew it.

'That's because you haven't heard what I have to say, yet,' she rasped.

His head tilted slightly to one side, his expression puzzled.

'You're angry.'

Ripping her gaze from his smiling, arching mouth, she hardened her heart.

'Scared,' she amended, sick to her stomach with nerves.

'Of me?' he asked, eyebrows arching in eloquent surprise.

'Of what you'll do.'

She gulped, her eyes filling with tears, and scowled down at her glass so that he didn't suspect that she was crying like a fool.

'But you know what I'm going to do,' he murmured.

Looking up quickly from under her lashes, she saw him smiling to himself as he contemplated his journey with Lio, perhaps his triumphant return and the happiness of being a father again.

But Lio needed someone sensitive to care for him, who'd devote time and patience to his needs—not a Lothario who breezed in and out of Lio's life merely to show off the evidence of his virility to his admiring friends.

'You must not take him!' she blurted out.

His eyes narrowed. 'Why not?' he asked quietly.

'You're not right for him!' she replied vehemently, her eyes clashing with his.

There was a silence so tense and profound that she could hear her heart beating and the clunk of the pendulum inside the grandfather clock that stood in the hall.

'Ah. What exactly has Linda told you about me?' he asked shrewdly.

'You were unfaithful,' Verity accused, blunt as ever. 'Over and over again! You neglected Linda and Lio for your women and for one in particular. Bianca. You were a rotten father and an even worse husband!' she flung.

'I see.' His tone was quiet. Subdued.

He didn't deny her accusations as she'd expected. She waited for an explanation, excuses, anything, but none came.

'And that's why you think I'm unsuitable to care for Lio,' he went on.

'Yes!' She was getting into her stride. 'But not *just* that—'

'Hmm. A category of complaints. I think we'd better start to unravel this. First, I need some information from you. What happened to Linda? How did she die?'

Did he care? she wondered bitterly. He'd been remarkably composed about his late wife's sudden death. Not a flicker of pain had crossed his face. Not a word of sorrow or regret.

Scornfully she met his piercing eyes, certain now that Vittore's infidelity had driven Linda to the edge and beyond. He'd effectively killed Linda. Ruined his own son.

'Her death was rather unpleasant,' she stated flatly.

She had his full attention. 'Tell me.'

So she drew in a huge breath and gave it to him cold. It was how she'd heard, after all. And he clearly didn't care.

'I was at home, in my flat the other side of London,' she said in a matter-of-fact tone. 'The police rang me. They'd found my name in Linda's diary which had been in her bag. There was nothing about you.'

'That doesn't surprise me,' he said. 'Go on.'

Her eyes met his and misery washed through her entire body. 'They said my sister had taken an overdose,' she whispered. 'And that she was dead.'

He started, his face drawn with shock. And then his head bowed low. Verity wondered if he was ashamed because he knew he had been largely responsible for Linda's state of mind. His hands covered his face and he let out a low groan.

'Linda!' he growled on a harsh outbreath.

Amazingly, she felt a surge of compassion for him and almost reached out to touch his arm. But not quite.

He had to know what damage he'd done by playing the field. Had to recognise that by being selfish you hurt people and caused them harm. Vittore should know that he mustn't play around with people's emotions and treat marriage so lightly, she thought angrily.

'There was a note,' she said, her voice shaking a little.

His eyes flicked up and she winced at the silver slashes of pain in them. 'Saying what?' he growled.

'Not much. That I was to look after Lio.' Being a witness to his distress was hurting her, and it shouldn't. Resentfully she muttered, 'The gist of it was that she couldn't go on.'

He muttered something in Italian. 'I can't believe it!' he exclaimed tightly. 'How could she leave her child?'

'I don't know,' Verity said honestly. 'But she must have been out of her mind with distress. Not only was she upset by your appalling behaviour, but—'

'*My* behaviour!' he exclaimed angrily. 'Let's get this straight. She left me over a year before she killed herself. I am not taking responsibility for her death. So what other reason was there? You seemed to be suggesting there was something else troubling her.'

Verity glared at the callous way he'd washed his hands of any blame. If he'd been half decent he would have made sure Linda had money of her own.

'Well, she was desperately in debt,' she said reluctantly. 'I imagine it was hard, living without support. There are hundreds of unpaid bills stuffed in her desk. I had to sort through them and I know that there was a huge loan on this house which had been unpaid for months, bills and demands from masseurs, a manicurist, personal trainer, credit card companies…' She bit her lip. 'Everything here was a sham—a lifestyle on borrowed money,' she said miserably. 'Poor Linda had got herself into serious financial trouble.'

'She could have come to me.' He frowned, his mouth bitter. 'Though she would have been obliged to let me see my son in return for financial assistance, wouldn't she?'

The man was impossible. He'd driven Linda away! He'd forced his wife and child into debt and misery! Verity winced, anger welling up within her till she could contain it no longer.

'You rat! You have no shame, no guilt—'

'No!' he cried, eyes blazing with a black fury. 'None!'

'At least we know where we stand,' Verity flared. 'You're not going to change your behaviour one iota—'

'I don't need to!'

'Right.' She folded her arms belligerently. 'Which brings us to Lio—'

'Yes! Exactly. Lio! Where the devil was he when Linda was overdosing?' he demanded. 'Was he left on his own? Was he afraid, hungry, abandoned?'

Vittore hurled the questions at her like a rocket, his whole body poised on the edge of the sofa as if he was ready to leap up and shake her if she didn't set his mind at rest.

'No. Someone was with him,' Verity said hastily. 'Linda was out. She was found unconscious in the powder room of a local club. But there was a babysitter in the house. A young girl from nearby. You don't think she'd leave her child alone, do you?' she asked indignantly.

'She has in the past. Nothing would surprise me,' he muttered.

'You're determined to cast Linda as the wicked witch, aren't you?' she shot.

'Just get on with the story.'

Her eyes flashed, her decision about Lio confirmed. She lifted her chin in a belligerent gesture and met his cynically mocking eyes without flinching.

'When the police rang to tell me what had happened, they were here in the house. I could hear a child screaming in the background. I realised it was Lio and came at once.

It took hours before I could calm him down. I've not left him since.'

'He must come back with me at once,' Vittore said with a frown. 'Away from this place that reminds him of his mother. He needs to begin a new life with me.'

'No!' she cried forcefully, petrified at the prospect. 'You can't just take him away! I won't let you! I *won't*!'

Vittore froze. Ruthless, lacerating eyes pinned her in her seat for daring to deny him what he wanted. She cringed. Oh, yes. She'd been right. Under the sexy charm, she thought, lay a will of pure steel.

He rose to his feet, blasting her with the full force of his anger.

'Can't I? *Watch me*!' he snarled.

She couldn't move for shock. And to her horror, he strode grim-faced towards the door while she sat there, paralysed, not able to do anything to stop him.

Suddenly, adrenaline rushed into her numbed body and she found herself vaulting awkwardly over the back of the easy chair where she'd been sitting.

Stark fear lent her wings and she managed to reach the door before he did, flinging herself at it and flattening her back against the solid mahogany, her arms spread wide in an attitude of defence.

'You've got to listen to me!' she pleaded desperately. 'You have to know *why* Lio must stay!'

The dark eyes were like chips of black ice. 'Don't make me hurt you, Verity,' he growled menacingly. 'Stand aside or I swear, I'll forget everything I ever learned about treating women with courtesy and I will pull you away by force and I won't care if I hurt you in the process. I've waited too long for this moment. Suffered too long. Nursed my hurt and my hatred till I thought I'd go insane, till my mother and my friends pulled me out of my despair and made me realise that I had to be ready for the day if I ever found Lio again.'

His voice grew husky and became so low in pitch that

she could hardly hear. It seemed to vibrate through her body at a low and insistent level, reaching her compassionate heart and finding easy entry.

'You can't imagine what it's been like for me all this time,' he continued throatily. 'Men aren't supposed to be enslaved by their children as women are. But I was, from the moment he was born, and neither you nor anyone on earth will keep me from him a moment longer!'

His hands closed around her arms as if to hurl her aside and she quickly grabbed the lapels of his jacket to bind him to her. Vittore's eyes flashed a warning. The heat of his chest burned into her flesh. The rock-hard solidity of him daunted her. But she meant to cling to him, limpet-like, Lio-like, till he listened.

'If you care about him you'll hear what I have to say! I keep trying to tell you! He's not *well*!' she yelled. And thus caught his attention.

'Very convenient. You said he *wasn't* ill just now,' he observed in an icy, disbelieving drawl.

Her senses were heightened by terror. She could feel the hot flurry of his breath, could inhale his delicious aftershave, found herself dizzy from the magnetic power of his burning eyes. Frantically she fought off the fog that threatened to descend on her brain.

'It's not physical. It's emotional. He's suffering from separation anxiety,' she gabbled. 'And it's serious.'

He searched her eyes and gradually realised she was telling the truth because a deep pain tautened her face, throwing the scimitar cheekbones into greater relief.

'Explain,' he rasped, his eyes bleak.

Thank heavens. Verity's eyes closed briefly and her hands slid from his lapels, down the hot solidity of his chest. He would listen, she thought, as he took a step back. And, because he cared about Lio, he wouldn't do anything to hurt him. Would he?

'Can we sit down?' she asked in a small voice. 'I'm so

tired I can barely stand. You'll understand why when I tell you.'

'*D'accordo,*' he rasped. 'Agreed.'

His hand slipped beneath her elbow. Carefully he helped her—not to the chair, but to the sofa, which he also occupied. At his raised eyebrow of grim encouragement, she nodded, found her glass and took a gulp of whisky then began.

'I don't know what went on here before Linda died,' she began, her voice shaking. Absently she curled her legs up under her, unconsciously making herself comfortable for the difficult explanation. 'Maybe Lio was perfectly normal when she was alive, maybe he wasn't. I've not found anyone around here who knew anything about him—'

'The babysitter?' he suggested, his expression grim.

Verity shook her head. 'The night of Linda's death was the first time the babysitter had been here—and she told me he'd been asleep when she'd arrived and he hadn't woken. Whatever Lio was like before, he has problems now. You must understand something, Vittore. He has latched on to me and won't let me out of his sight. A lot of the time he's physically attached to me in one way or another. If he feels safe, then he'll play a short distance away. But strangers worry him, and I can't go anywhere without him running after me.'

'What happens if you're out of his sight?'

'He screams,' she said simply.

'Is that all?' Vittore exclaimed. He shook his head as if her methods left a lot to be desired. 'If he yells out of sheer obstinacy, or has a tantrum, then the common practice is to ignore such bad behaviour,' he said firmly. 'You don't reward anti-social conduct by giving it your attention.'

'It's not a tantrum!' she cried in exasperation. 'When you hear him, you'll realise that. It's sheer terror. It's pitiful. It wrenches at my heart. Oh, I know this must not be what you want to hear, and I'm sorry to dash your hopes, but I'm convinced that Lio will go crazy if I disappear out of his life, just like his mother did. Think of it. One day his mother was there, then he woke and found that he was confronted by total strangers.'

'And just over a year ago, one day his father was there and then Lio found he was in another house, another country,' Vittore pointed out bitterly.

'I know,' she agreed. 'His life has been fractured, to say the least. But when Linda died he must have felt totally abandoned by the one person he really knew.'

Vittore bit his lip, bleakness deepening the hollows of his face and dulling his eyes. 'Poor child,' he growled under his breath. 'What a mess.'

Verity felt the sympathy return despite her dislike of him. She sighed heavily.

'It is. If you'd been there, I suppose he would have clung to you, but you weren't. It happened to be me he turned to. I represent the only security he knows,' she said earnestly. 'We can't take that from him, can we? He's the important one in this, not us. Our wishes are unimportant. Lio comes first. I've no idea what we're going to do, but that's the situation. And for Lio's sake, I beg you to respect his needs. You *can't* take him away while he's like this! It would be too cruel!'

To her astonishment and irritation, Vittore smiled gently, the light returning to his eyes.

'I don't think you realise, Verity,' he said softly. 'Children respond very well to me—'

'Not in this case!' she declared, dismayed that he hadn't realised the seriousness of Lio's insecurity.

'You'll see,' he told her cheerfully. 'I am very fond of children. And of course I love Lio very much. After a short time—an hour or two, he will be at ease with me and everything will be all right. Don't worry about him. I am sure I can handle him.'

She groaned in exasperation and scrambled to her knees. 'You don't get it, do you? This isn't some little upset he's had. He's traumatised. You're *wrong*!' she protested desperately.

'No! You are!' His angry tone and the stop sign he made with his hand had a horrible finality about them. 'Now it is your turn to listen. Lio is my son and I love him. There's nothing more to say about the matter. Because of what you have said, I will not take him now but I will wait until the morning when he and I can make friends—'

'But—!'

'However,' he rolled on regardless, 'I will stay here tonight. I, too, cannot risk him being snatched from under my nose—'

'I wouldn't do that!' she flung indignantly.

'No? You seem very passionate, very determined to prevent me from bonding with my child,' he observed, dark eyes reproving her.

'Bond if you can!' she hurled, knowing he wouldn't. He'd see the extent of the problem in the morning. Then he'd have to concede defeat. 'Be my guest,' she added bitterly.

'Your guest? This is my house,' he pointed out sharply. 'At least, the debt is mine. *You* are the guest. And in the morning, you will pack his things—and Linda's bills and papers—and when he and I have played together for a short while, we will then fly to Italy.'

'And if he won't play?'

'We go. That's final.'

She stared in horror. 'But...you can't do that! And...Italy! I—I wouldn't ever s-see him!' she stuttered, utterly appalled that Vittore meant to ignore everything she'd said.

She'd be miles away from Lio and he'd be crying his heart out, lost and scared... Her face crumpled, misery welling up to choke her.

'It's not that far away. You can visit,' Vittore said, quite gently as if he recognised the extent of her affection and felt sorry for her. 'You are his aunt and therefore will always be welcome. My mother would like to meet you, I'm sure. And whatever you say to the contrary, you will be properly thanked for what you have done. Tomorrow you can get on with your life,' he soothed, patting her bare thigh consolingly, 'which I am sure has been put on hold for the past two months.'

Words failed her. Numb with disbelief, she gazed blearily up at him, so overwhelmed by tears that she couldn't argue her case any further.

'Please don't cry,' he said gently.

'I'm not crying!' she raged, stupidly denying the obvious and crossly catching up the salty drops with her tongue as if that might hide them.

'I understand that this is difficult for you,' he murmured, voice, hands and eyes combining to placate her. 'You've looked after him for many weeks and have become attached to him—'

'Attached isn't the right word,' she muttered miserably. 'Super-glued is closer.'

'We both know he has to come back to Italy with me,' Vittore went on relentlessly. *'Tomorrow.'*

'No—!'

'Excuse me,' he said, his manner short and sharp. 'I want to look at him again and then I will collect my overnight bag from my hire car and find somewhere to sleep.'

He strode to the door. She opened her mouth to protest but nothing came out other than a choking cry. For a moment she heard his steps falter and then they quickened and faded.

Unbelievably distressed, Verity slumped in a heap, sobbing her heart out for baby Lio and for herself.

In a few hours the light of her life would be gone. All too vividly she could picture the scene tomorrow: Lio, screaming at being parted from her, fear and hysteria in his eyes, his body rigid with terror.

'No!' she whispered sickly.

The image was too painful to bear and she pressed her

hands against her face in an effort to obliterate it. She felt quite desolate. Vittore's plan was brutal. Anything could happen to Lio's fragile emotions. *Anything*.

She would stop Vittore. She didn't know how, only that she must. Tormented and racked with misery, she wept uncontrollably for her little nephew, terrified that Vittore's insensitive handling would be the ruin of little Lio.

CHAPTER FOUR

In a state of euphoria, Vittore stripped off his clothes and took a shower, then slipped naked into the bed in the nursery, beside Lio's cot. For a while he lay propped up on one arm, watching his sleeping son with deep love filling his heart.

'Sleep on, my little one. We'll be together from now on,' he said softly.

There would be no problems. Lio needed the love, security and skills that he—as a doting father—possessed. For all her good intentions and sincerity, Verity clearly didn't know how to handle children. She wore no ring, presumably had little experience of toddlers.

Contentedly, he settled down to sleep. He'd show her how it was done and she'd have to concede that he'd manage Lio very well.

'See you in the morning, *son*,' he whispered happily, and closed his eyes in blissful contentment.

His life had begun again. He felt a pure joy entering every cell, filling him with vibrant energy and an eagerness for the future. The women in his life would adore Lio. He smiled, imagining their faces, and settled down contentedly for the night, happier than he'd been for a long time.

And yet, perhaps it was the stifling heat of the summer night, or the eventful past hours, but he found it impossible to sleep. Tossing and turning for a couple of hours, he found his mind leaping erratically.

He was picturing his mother's face when he returned with Lio—since he hadn't told her why he was flying to England in case of disappointment—when up popped the face of the intense and passionate Verity, who had seemed determined to thwart him at every step.

From that moment on, she and Lio filled his thoughts to the exclusion of all else. He could visualise them in such detail that it was almost as if they'd been imprinted on his brain cells.

And then, on hearing a soft, rustling sound, he opened his eyes—and to his astonishment, there she was!

Intrigued, he sat up sharply in bed, something odd about her movements stopping him from speaking to her.

In a thin, semi-transparent nightdress that bared her lovely shoulders and the first swell of her breasts, she walked quietly towards the cot. Not once did she glance in his direction, though she must have realised he was there because the night-light shed a soft glow over the whole room.

Silver tracks marked her mournful face where tears had cascaded down her cheeks. Her lashes fluttered wet and spiky around her watery-violet eyes and every now and then a stray sob escaped her trembling lips. Vittore was transfixed, the breath catching in his throat.

He remembered the feel of her bare thigh beneath his hand when he had soothed her. The clarity of her incredible eyes, the tempting softness of her lush mouth that had constantly captured his gaze and forced him to acknowledge that celibacy was, perhaps, not an option for his future life after all.

And now she had come to his room. He swallowed. Had she come to plead her case? If so, she was playing with fire to be so flimsily dressed—unless that had been intentional.

'Verity—'

He stopped. She didn't acknowledge him. Clearly deeply unhappy, she settled herself down on the floor beside the cot. To his amazement, she curled up as if to sleep.

Vittore stared, baffled by her behaviour. Was this a gesture of defiance? Didn't she trust his word?

The curve of her arm supporting her tousled head looked touchingly sweet. The line of her thigh aroused more primitive urges within him. What the devil was she trying to do to him?

'Verity,' he said sternly. She didn't move. 'Verity!'

He saw that her breathing had become deep and regular, the tantalising cleavage dark between her crushed breasts as they rose and fell rhythmically.

She couldn't have fallen asleep. The sexual tensions between them were too obvious, too fierce, for her to judge this a safe situation. She was pretending, perhaps hoping he'd touch her…

As he must. Nothing would keep him from her. Even now, he was sliding out of bed, his heart leaping, his long-denied body hot with hunger.

'Verity,' he murmured, stroking her face.

She didn't flinch, didn't betray herself with even a flicker of an eyelid. If he didn't know better, he would have said that she was fast asleep, her face relaxed, her moist lips drowsy. Smiling, he touched her mouth with his forefinger, which he then brought to his own lips. And tasted salt.

Her pulse felt even beneath his questing fingers. When he tentatively lifted one arm, it seemed limp.

She *was* asleep!

It dawned on him then that she could have been sleepwalking. A feeling of intense tenderness swept over him. Startled by this, he went back to the bed, removed a pillow and the counterpane which he had discarded, and arranged them slowly, carefully, for her so that she slept more comfortably.

In doing so, he touched her body as he moved it. Felt its yielding softness, inhaled the faint drift of natural perfume on her skin.

Fatal. His fingers lingered, his eyes feasted. An extraordinary feeling came over him, a sweet sensation of exaltation mingled with raw, naked desire that fired him to fever pitch.

He wanted her. Or, at least, his starved body did. He groaned, and tried to rein in his hot-blooded desire to pick her up and take her off to her own bed before slowly, beautifully, kissing that plush mouth and that luscious body and making slow and passionate love to her all night long.

Annoyed by his lurching emotions, Vittore got between his own sheets again and did all the usual things to crush the unwelcome desire. A review of his stocks and shares. Complicated mathematics and half-remembered formulae from his schooldays.

Somewhere around the mental listing of the staff in his Turin factory and the five hundred retail outlets worldwide, he finally won his battle with his foolhardy lust and fell asleep.

When he woke, it was a moment before he remembered where he was. He glanced at his watch. Six-thirty. Might as well start the day.

Rolling over, he expected—hoped—to see Verity fast asleep on the floor, but she had gone. The counterpane and the pillow had been pushed to one side.

'*Madonna!*' he rasped, suddenly alarmed.

A quick glance fed his fears. *Lio wasn't there!*

In a flash he'd scrambled out of bed, frantically hauled on some boxer shorts and hurtled from room to room like a whirlwind, desperately searching for his son.

One bedroom was clearly Verity's. The nightdress lay abandoned on the bed, the room seemed to be in chaos, as if…

His spine chilled. As if she'd flung things around, hastily packing perhaps…

'Verity!' he yelled, leaping to the head of the stairs. *'Verity!'*

This wasn't happening to him. Not again. She hadn't, surely, taken Lio… He let out a hoarse, feral cry and his feet thundered down the staircase as he bounded two, three, steps at a time with scant regard for his safety. Nothing mattered. Only Lio. Let him be in time! If she'd gone…

'Verity!' he bellowed, raging, desperate, wild-eyed and despairing.

'What on earth…?'

He skidded to a stop. Swallowed back the nausea, the cloying emotion, the misery. Felt waves of relief crash through his agonised body. Offered up heartfelt thanks and leaned against a pillar, shaking.

She stood in the doorway of what must be the kitchen and blinking at the sight of his bare chest and legs. She looked startled. And to his relieved eyes, stunningly beautiful. An ache formed where his heart beat frantically in his heaving ribcage.

Something, someone, whimpered. Moist-eyed, he looked down and saw that Lio's arms were wrapped tightly around Verity's legs and his son was peering around her slender thigh nervously.

Assailed by a pang of tenderness and joy, he saw that Lio's eyes were almost peacock blue and they were awash with tears, the small rosebud mouth quivering with trepidation.

'It's all right, sweetheart,' Verity said in cheerful, reassuring tones as she stroked the white-blond hair with tender caresses. 'What a lot of noise! All that banging about and stamping down the stairs! We thought it was a big teddy bear coming for breakfast, didn't we? Wasn't it fun?'

Lio's trembling lip made it clear that he didn't think it had been fun at all. Vittore was grateful to her for trying.

'I thought… I thought you'd taken him away,' he explained, panting heavily.

Her eyes widened indignantly. 'I said I wouldn't!' she hissed, *sotto voce*.

'Your room… I looked in… it looked as if you'd tried to pack in a hurry—'

'I'm untidy,' she said tightly. 'I don't have time to be

neat. How could you, Vittore? You've upset him. Frightened him. Well done. So much for your sensitivity!'

She scooped Lio up and murmured soothingly to him, jogging him up and down. Then she disappeared into the kitchen and Vittore could hear her singing breathlessly. There was a child's giggle and Vittore heaved a heavy, despairing sigh.

He was the child's father. He'd wanted to meet Lio with a smile, to say 'Hello, Lio! I am your Papa!' And now... Sweet heaven, he wanted his son. His arms ached for his child.

His fist slammed into his palm. He'd have to work very hard to gain his son's confidence. *Curse* it.

After a moment he had composed himself and risked walking into the room. Verity was dancing around, dipping and swaying, in an attempt to banish Lio's fears with her jollity. Vittore watched her enviously. And yearned to have his son in his empty embrace.

Lio wore a navy and white striped top which brought out the deep colour of his eyes and looked wonderful with his blond hair. His navy shorts seemed touchingly baggy on his thin legs and Vittore felt his heart bump hard in his chest.

Was Lio undernourished? Toddlers weren't usually that slender, were they? He opened his mouth to comment and found himself closing it again after a warning glare from Verity.

She couldn't believe how clumsy Vittore had been. He'd really ruined any chance of a gentle and subtle introduction to Lio! Her fears had been confirmed. He had no idea at all how careful he'd have to be.

'Did you...sleep well?' Vittore asked casually.

She blinked at the extraordinary question. Her night had been disturbed with kaleidoscopic dreams and she felt as stiff as if she'd slept on a concrete floor, but that was none of his business.

'Just stay quiet, Vittore,' she said, keeping her voice

neutral for Lio's sake. Vittore looked like a pirate with that dark, sexy stubble. Enough to scare any child. Though it did peculiar things to her. 'So, sweetheart! Shall we have our bacon now? Mmm! Scrummy!' She smacked her lips and Lio copied, making her laugh. 'Into your chair…yes, in you go! It's OK, I'm here, I'm holding you, look how close I am! Snuggle close. Kiss close. Mmm! That's a good boy. Now. We'll eat together, one for you…one for me… Sit down and make yourself smaller instead of looming like a giant who's lost his beanstalk,' she murmured in Vittore's direction, keeping up the merry tone.

And then she decided that she couldn't cope with an expanse of muscular torso and shapely male calves and thighs over the cornflakes. It was playing havoc with her blood pressure.

'On second thoughts, go and get some clothes on. You'll curdle the milk,' she ordered.

She heard him release a sharp, irritated breath. And then he was leaving the room, Lio's apprehensive eyes following his father, the child's mobile mouth quivering uncertainly.

It seemed as if someone had taken the pressure valve off the atmosphere. Only then did she realise how tense she felt when Vittore was around.

'Idiot,' she told herself.

And doubled her entertainment level, managing to get some food into Lio before Vittore appeared again. When he did, Lio whined and reached up to be held. Resigned, she lifted him onto her lap and gave him his non-spill cup.

She looked across at Vittore and instantly felt as if she'd been plugged into a battery charger. All he was doing, was sitting there; silently watching his son. But he looked gorgeous, his olive skin gleaming and freshly shaven. His white shirt could have taken a leading part in a washing powder advert and his elegantly cut stone suit flattered every inch of his body.

But it was something more intangible that actually affected her deeply—a chemistry that altered her from a mature, self-sufficient woman into a gibbering idiot the minute he came within fifty feet of her. Stick a bit of litmus paper on her, and she'd turn scarlet and ignite, she thought gloomily.

And now he was turning his dark, bitter-chocolate eyes on her as if puzzled by something—as if, she thought, her eyes widening, he too wondered at the strange energy field which flowed between them.

Though she doubted that *his* brains felt as if they were whirling about like a windmill in a force ten gale.

He frowned and the tip of his tongue moistened his lips. In response, a quiver rippled through every nerve she possessed. Down went his lashes to hide his eyes.

He sucked in a breath and then his gaze shifted to his son. Vittore's stunned expression changed, the lines of strain on his face smoothing out into a tender smile.

'*Ciao bambino.* Hello, little man,' he said, very softly.

And his smile was so loving that Verity felt her heart turn over. She didn't know whether to be sad or relieved when Lio whimpered and buried his head in her chest. Sad, she decided. For Lio, for his father. Automatically she stroked the soft, baby hair and murmured soothingly.

'It's Daddy! Hello, Daddy,' she said encouragingly.

'Papa,' Vittore corrected, sounding very croaky.

She nodded and lifted Lio away but he began to grizzle and kick, reaching for the safety of her bosom, pulling the neckline of her sundress out of shape.

'Put him down,' Vittore said with a frown.

She glared at him, secured her hold on Lio and stood up, rocking the fretful, distressed child till he was calm again.

'If I had put him down,' she then said quietly, trying not to sound as angry as she felt, 'he would have screamed and screamed and crawled towards me blindly, pathetically, to grab any part of me he could. You must realise. Lio is not being naughty. He's genuinely insecure and needs loads and loads of love, not cold-hearted, logic-based man-management!'

Vittore's mouth thinned and she felt a pang of sympathy. It must be dreadful, being a stranger to your own child. A frightening stranger, at that!

'This isn't going as I'd hoped,' he rasped.

'I did warn you,' she said gently. 'You won't take him when he's like this, will you?'

He heaved a heavy sigh. 'No. May I make myself some coffee?' he asked.

'Of course. Go carefully, no sudden movements.' She hesitated, her tender heart reaching out to him in his plight. 'Give it time, Vittore.'

'How long? An hour? A day, a week?'

She looked down at the clinging Lio. Who could say? And maybe Vittore would give up after a while and return to his playboy life. Then she'd be left in peace with Lio—and she'd get her body back into order. Some perverse part of her, however, objected strongly to that scenario.

She was attracted to him, she thought in dismay. Her first real crush—and it had to be Lio's father!

'I don't know, Vittore,' she whispered, seeing he was waiting for her answer. 'I honestly have no idea.'

Prowling up and down the kitchen a week later, Vittore felt close to letting out a roar of frustration. His movements were mechanical as he gathered the ingredients for supper. Cooking was the one thing he could do to help Verity.

He banged down some chicken thighs and smeared them with honey and herbs, suddenly afraid that Lio would never break away from Verity's skirts. It broke his heart to see his own son so terribly frightened of him.

Dio! He couldn't take much more, he thought desperately. His son should be happy and normal, creating chaos and laughter and exasperation in every corner of the house.

Instead, Lio clung to Verity and barely left her alone for a moment. Angrily Vittore chopped vegetables, trying not to think of Lio's distress. It hurt so much. And every second of every day he blessed Verity for being around to pick up the pieces of his son's sanity and for remaining so calm and patient despite her exhaustion.

He looked up, hearing her coming down the stairs with that slow, weary thump he now recognised as evidence of her shattering day.

She stood swaying in the doorway, her hair dishevelled, face soft and vulnerable, body utterly womanly in the long, clinging dress that matched her incomparable eyes and enriched their drowsy depths.

'Have some wine,' he offered.

'My saviour,' she sighed and took the chair he held out for her.

Crumpled, tousled and utterly irresistible, she sat down and listlessly watched him pour the wine into a crystal glass.

'Took a long time tonight,' he commented sympathetically, lighting candles to keep his hands occupied. How long had she been up there? Over an hour and a half, certainly.

He wanted to go to her. Fold her in his embrace and give…and take, sweet heaven, to take!…comfort from the human contact. But knew his emotions were too close to the surface to be kept in control if he allowed himself such an indulgence.

Verity's huge, sad eyes looked at him over the rim of her glass. She sipped her wine and when she put her drink back on the table her lips were moist and glistening. Vittore felt his heart-rate shoot up. And busied himself with grilling the peppers.

'He was very tired but wouldn't close his eyes,' she sighed. 'I read four stories and sang virtually all the quiet and gentle songs I know.' She yawned and stretched, then flopped back into a slump. 'I think I could go to bed now.'

He smiled at her. 'It wouldn't be the first time you've fallen asleep over your meal.'

'I know. He was awful today, wasn't he? Poor little scrap.'

Vittore bent his head to hide his misery. He'd tried everything. Buying a toy haybaler and a huge digger—which he himself had played with enthusiastically, meanwhile ignoring Lio in the hope that the kiddie would be tempted. Making music out of saucepan lids and spoons and partly-filled bottles. Playing 'Boo!' from behind the trees.

No response. Nothing. Just tears. And whenever Verity took one pace too many away from Lio, he'd launch into a frenzy of hysterical screaming that had chilled Vittore's very bones and made his heart weep for his unhappy, muddled little baby.

'I think he needs help,' he said huskily.

'Love,' she answered. 'Love and routine and security.'

'We all need that.'

He couldn't understand why his voice was so croaky. Emotion was welling up, ruining his determination to master this situation. Not only was he having to contend with his son's misery, but the intimacy of hour after hour, day after day with Verity was driving him insane with desire.

Tight-lipped, desperate to keep the lid on his chaotic emotions, he reduced life to basic banalities. Checking the oven. Turning the peppers. Pouring more wine.

Meeting her soft eyes. Watching the dark lashes flutter tiredly, the gentle mouth drooping with exhaustion.

'I did see the doctor,' she mumbled. 'He recommended love and security and to come back in three months if there were still problems.'

'We'll talk about it another time. Supper's nearly ready,' he said. 'Stay awake.'

Her lips parted in a faint smile. 'I'll try. It smells gorgeous. Like a Mediterranean summer.' Her eyes met his with a melting warmth and he felt his hand shaking as he struggled to pick up the chicken with the tongs. 'Thanks. I'm really grateful.'

'Prego,' he said automatically. 'You're welcome,' he

translated, mesmerised by the slow movement of her mouth. 'Here we are.'

Carefully he ladled some of the aromatic mixture onto her plate and took a deep breath before placing it in front of her. The way he felt, anything closer than a table's breadth was dangerously inflammatory.

She took an exploratory bite. 'Mmm!' she sighed. 'Chicken's divine. Tender and succulent. How do you do it? You're not exactly domesticated, are you?'

He laughed ruefully. His other attempts to help her had been disastrous. Consequently when Lio had his daytime sleep it was she who rushed about dealing with the washing and ironing and essential house-cleaning.

'Never had to do anything domestic in my life,' he admitted.

'You filled the freezer and the fridge,' she reminded him, taking an appreciative bite from a hot, crusty roll. 'It's wonderful, having such a choice of exciting food.'

'I wish I could do more.'

Much more. He imagined her teeth grazing his chest, her fingers running over his body…

'I wish you could, too,' she giggled, perking up a little. 'But I think that having Lio in shrunken purple bibs, T-shirts, shorts and socks with me in mini-sized purple shirts, underwear and hankies, is taking downsizing and colour co-ordination too far!'

He laughed and looked apologetic. He'd been banned from the washing machine after that. 'I wanted to surprise you—'

'And succeeded!' She grinned, her smile friendly. 'I know you were trying to help. It's not your fault that people have run around you all your life. How did you ever learn to cook?'

'The housekeeper. Maria. From childhood on, I spent hours in the kitchen. It was a noisy, bustling place, full of visitors and children and I loved it. She fed me titbits and I fetched things for her then she taught me to cook.'

Verity raised her glass. 'Thanks, Maria!' she said fervently. She pushed back her heavily hanging hair with a weary hand, the sweep of her arm both graceful and seductive. 'If she hadn't taught you, if you hadn't been here, I would have been munching a bag of crisps and following that up with a bar of chocolate and galloping acne.'

He could have taken her in his arms there and then. Brought her to life with demanding kisses, promising her an easier life as his mistress. But she wasn't ready for him yet, and he wanted her to be driven mad by him. That was what he wanted from her. Unbridled, uninhibited wantonness.

'You seem more tired every day that passes,' he said quietly.

'I am. It's getting worse. I don't seem to sleep well.'

'No,' he breathed and cleared his throat.

Every night she came to the nursery where he slept. She'd sleepwalk in and check Lio and sometimes turn around and leave immediately. Other times she'd sit on his bed and she'd be so close that he could make out the perfect line of her spine beneath the thin nightdress, and the seductive curve of her hips.

Once she had curled up on the end of the bed and stayed for half an hour, leaving him bathed in a thin film of sweat.

He had to do something or go mad. He wanted Lio more desperately than ever. Seeing him daily and not touching him was breaking his heart in two. And his helpless lust for Verity wasn't helping.

It would be different if they were in Italy, he thought gloomily, pushing his plate away. He paused. Yes. Why not?

He looked across at her where she sat slowly nibbling a strip of pepper, her eyes distant and dreamy. The last piece of scarlet pepper slid into her mouth and she absently licked the fingers that had been holding it. He felt a strong curl of desire rolling through his body.

A plan began to form in his mind. Excitement lifted his spirits. He could have it all. His eyes sparkled.

'I admire you for what you have done for Lio,' he said huskily.

Verity's huge violet eyes fastened on his and she blushed.

'I couldn't help it,' she dismissed. 'I'd do anything for him,' she added in a sad whisper.

Despite trying not to, he found himself gazing at the swell of her breasts where they rose and fell rapidly above the deep neckline. His pulses raced. The atmosphere seemed thick with sexual tension as their eyes met and the heat pumped inexorably between them.

It was obvious that she was aroused. Confused by her feelings, too. Her hands were twisting together. She didn't like what was happening to her. No matter. That would be easy to change. Sexual desire invariably rode roughshod over rational thought.

The plan he'd devised would appeal to her, even though she might feel obliged to object. They had more than one reason to stay together: Lio, and an all-consuming desire for one another. In the end, she'd fall in with his suggestion. All his worries could be over, and he would have what he wanted most: his son, and the captivating Verity.

He smiled at her, exulting in the unspoken promise of her answering, trembling smile and her subsequent confusion when she stabbed her fork repeatedly at the rim of her plate as if she wasn't aware of what she was doing.

Simmering with a secret triumph, he forced himself to eat his own meal in the heavy, sensual silence that boiled and coiled around them.

Her mouth seemed to be dry because she licked her lips often. So did he—and wished his mouth was on hers, moistening it, feeding on it.

He shifted in his chair uncomfortably and noticed that she kept adjusting her position, too. Somehow he stifled a groan and stopped his hands reaching out to imprison her face and hold it till he had kissed every silken inch.

To his increasing delight, she ate little of her pudding, scooping up minute forkfuls of the individual pear crumble with a shaking hand that somehow just managed to find her nervously parted lips.

He'd never felt so wired up before. Explosions of excitement were bursting inside him, stoking up his pulses to a frantic pace.

'You don't like it?' he rasped hoarsely, when she stared helplessly at the pudding she'd hardly touched.

'It's...delicious,' she whispered.

He cleared his throat. 'Then why...?'

Verity didn't look up. As if ashamed, she put down her fork with a clatter and pressed her lips together hard.

'No reason.'

'Don't pretend. It's nothing to be ashamed of. We're adults. Free agents.'

'I don't know what you mean,' she said slowly.

'You feel it, too,' he said softly. 'It consumes you. Stops you eating. Takes over your mind. Yes?'

She looked appalled but the rapidity of her breathing answered him. In the candlelight she looked very vulnerable. Unstoppable passion soared through his veins and he couldn't hold back. His hand had reached out to enclose hers and they were staring into each other's eyes as if they'd never seen one another before.

His lips pressed against her fingers, feeling them flutter. More boldly, he took her thumb and slowly, painfully sweetly, drew its length into his mouth before releasing it. She gave a satisfying little whimper that set his body aflame.

'Verity,' he murmured, long and slow, the name liquid on his tongue.

The lagoon eyes widened and he felt a kick of something fierce and sharp in his stomach, like a thunderbolt landing.

Verity didn't know what was happening to her. Only

that she couldn't move, couldn't speak, could hardly breathe. Vittore's suppressed energy swamped her, filling her tired body with life—and an inexplicable joy.

In the back of her mind she knew what he intended. If she'd made the effort, she could have snatched her hand away perhaps, or announced she was dead on her feet and was going to bed, but she wanted him to kiss her so badly that she let the wonderful mist invade her brain, let the fires within her kindle and ignite and sat there waiting, hoping, squirming in delicious anticipation.

Suddenly he was beside her chair, his movements liquid and flowing. Drawing her to her feet. She flung back her head and let out a small gasp because her breath was almost choking her.

There was a soft warmth on her throat, the slide of his mouth sending rivers of pleasure through her entire body. She whispered nonsense, loving it, fearing it, unable to understand why the touch of his lips should fling her so far and so quickly into uncontainable rapture.

His thumb firmly tipped down her chin. And then his mouth descended on hers; firm, sweet, gently impassioned, as if he enjoyed luxuriating in the erotic feel of her lips and would do so for the next hour.

But she wanted more. Now. Why not?

'Vittore!' she moaned, wrapping her limbs around his.

And she was being borne back, to the wall, the pressure of his body hard and thrilling, the frail, tenuous clutch that she had on reality slowly seeping away with every fevered kiss, every tormenting caress of his expert hands that teased and delighted every sense she possessed and spun them to heights she'd never dreamed possible.

Madness was unfurling inside her, rocketing to fill every part of her body as she clawed and begged and groaned for him to satisfy her intense and unbearable hunger.

His mouth swooped to her breasts and she—shy, virginal, modest—flung her head back with a cry of release, proud of their taut fullness and thinking that she might die of pleasure as his mouth closed on each swollen bud in turn, suckling, rubbing, kissing…

Outrageously, she revelled in the feel of him. The softness of his shirt. The rock wall of his powerful chest beneath. The smell of his hair. The strength of his arms and narrowness of his waist. The way he looked at her; drowsily, feverishly, a little astounded by what had happened.

There was an incredible hard ridge of warmth against her loins and something leapt inside her, a ripple of nerves sighing with delight. The core of her body pounded like a pulsating furnace, urging her on to uncharacteristic wantonness.

'Touch me,' she moaned, astonished that she could be so bold. But she was incapable of remaining merely acquiescent. 'Vittore…*touch* me!'

CHAPTER FIVE

VITTORE groaned from deep within his chest, then kissed her hard and long, the shuddering of his body and the blaze in his brilliant eyes eloquently conveying to her the fever that consumed him.

Frantically he pushed her a little higher up the wall, his mouth once more avidly devoted to her straining breasts. Shockingly, she lifted first one, then the other to his searching lips, whimpering at the sensations which sliced delicious channels within her, the spasms fiercer and harder with every tug of his mouth and every second she gazed dazedly at his lowered lashes and impassioned face.

Then came the heat of his hand searing her thigh, sliding her dress up further and further. Strung high with anticipation, she grabbed his head and kissed him with all the force she could muster, gasping when his tongue curled with hers and began to thrust in an invasion that echoed something even more intimate.

She struggled, pushing him back, craving more. She couldn't wait. Couldn't bear it any longer.

'Please, Vittore!' she quavered, furious that he was taking so long to satisfy her.

A lyrical stream of Italian whispered harshly from his hot lips. His fingers had found the lace edge of her small panties and were easing them down.

And then the beautiful language began to have some meaning to her fuddled brain. In a flash she came to her senses. Italian, she thought, her mind clearing sharply. This is Vittore. Womaniser. Adulterer. Not the man to be trusted with her virginity, however desperate she was to give it to him.

Utterly in tune with her, he paused at the stiffening of her body, rocking on his feet.

'Verity?' he growled.

Her eyes closed in horror at what she'd nearly done. And at what she'd already allowed. Frantically she wriggled away and slithered to the ground—though her legs wouldn't hold her and for the moment she had to let him grasp her waist to keep her upright.

'I—' Scarlet, she saw her shamefully naked breasts and awkwardly slid her straps up her arms to make herself decent again. She couldn't continue. For several seconds she had to fight her hunger and find her voice. 'I had too much wine,' she fudged feebly.

'Hardly any,' he muttered, frighteningly satanic, his eyes glitteringly black.

'More than enough.' She took a tentative step to the side, found she could just manage a stumble or two, and lurched towards a chair where she sat shaking; horribly, desperately frustrated. Every pore throbbed. Every cell screamed at her for satisfaction. And she wanted to scream, too, because she'd been so stupid. 'I don't know what came over me,' she whispered.

'I do.'

She flung him a baleful glare. 'You're not helping!'

'I don't feel inclined to!' he bit.

'I'm sorry. I got carried away,' she said stiffly.

'Not far enough,' he said with vicious regret. He drew in a huge breath and to her alarm, came over to crouch beside the chair. 'Verity,' he said huskily, his hand on her knee. 'No. Listen,' he grated, when she jerked back in concern. 'Why did you stop?' he asked in a hoarse whisper.

She set her jaw, hunting for strength and composure. Her eyes were troubled when they met his.

'Sanity prevailed. I don't do one-night stands,' she answered flatly.

His finger brushed a strand of wayward hair from her

face. When he curled the strand around her ear, she shivered with pleasure, his touch electrifying her again.

And he must have known that because he smiled lazily, his eyes once more drowsy with desire.

'It needn't be like that,' he said in a low tone that throbbed with excitement.

What was he suggesting? Two nights? Three? Something raw and visceral burrowed its way insistently in the depths of her being. Miserable that her body was starting to betray her, she turned her head away and tried to stand. But he pushed her back in the chair.

'What the hell are you doing?' she flared, privately panicking.

'Stopping you from rushing off. I have the solution to our problem about Lio,' he replied easily.

She frowned, confused by his change of tack. Her mind was working too lethargically to understand. 'What?'

'I worked it out earlier this evening.'

His hand rested on her knee, his thumb rhythmically stroking. He seemed a little tense but perfectly in control of himself, as if he was able to turn his passion on and off without effort. She bristled, annoyed. No man had promised her ecstasy before, let her taste it—and then calmly accepted her rejection.

She tried to be indifferent too. 'Worked out what?'

'The solution. Let's establish one or two things. First, you agree that Lio should know his father, yes?'

'Ye-e-es.' She took a deep breath. 'Yes, of course. I've never denied that.'

She looked wary. What was he up to? Why had he abandoned the idea of seducing her when he must know that she had almost surrendered? Why wasn't he kissing her, demanding…oh, God! she groaned silently. She felt so empty. And hated him and herself for being ruled by basic instincts.

'Good.' His thumb travelled a little further up her thigh. She clamped her hand on his, pushing it away. He made no protest and she found herself watching his fingers, wondering, wishing… 'Now,' he said, making her jump with his brusque efficiency. 'The situation is this. I need to return to Italy to deal with my business. There's only so much I can do by telephone and e-mail.'

'Oh.'

He smiled and she hoped he hadn't detected the note of disappointment in her response. Of course she wanted him to go. Probably. Except…

Annoyed with her stupid vacillating, she whipped her brain sternly into order. 'You go, then,' she said smartly.

Or at least, she'd intended to sound brisk. Her voice had been more rasping, as if, she thought gloomily, she'd smoked forty a day for the past twenty years. And he was smiling a knowing smile, the kind of smug, 'I've got you where I want you' kind of smile. She really must try harder, she scowled.

'One problem. I won't leave without Lio,' he stated. 'And he won't go anywhere without you.'

'No,' she agreed, trying not to drown in his wide, chocolate-dark eyes. 'Stalemate,' she pronounced. 'Something has to give. I think it'll have to be you.'

'I don't think so.'

He looked horribly self-satisfied and she sat up in her chair, suddenly alert. Her worst fears had come true!

'I won't leave him!' she declared furiously. 'You can't part us—!'

'You won't have to,' Vittore soothed.

'But…how—?'

'It's simple. You will both come with me. We go tonight, while he's asleep to minimise his distress—'

'*Whaaat?* But—!'

'I have arranged everything. It's settled. We'll fling his clothes and favourite toys into cases,' he forged on inexorably. 'A chauffeured car will pick us up in an hour and we'll be on my private jet and in Naples airport before you know it.' His eyes gleamed, his voice purred with pleasure.

'You see, Verity, this is the perfect solution to all our needs!'

All? Did he mean...? Her mouth fell open in astonishment. Then snapped shut again, this time in anger.

'Oh, I see! So that's what you were doing just now!' she hurled shakily. 'Softening me up! Organising dinner by candlelight, plenty of wine, taking advantage of my exhaustion to half-seduce me so I'd eagerly fall in with your plans!'

'Verity, I—'

'And then, presumably, you thought I'd not only be willing to look after Lio, but I'd be a useful little bedmate tucked away in your house, whenever you wanted a bit of slap and tickle! Oh, yes, your needs would be well catered for! A substitute mother by day and a whore at night! How *dare* you?' she raged, incensed that he could be so cold-blooded as to coax her in such a way—when she'd stupidly imagined he'd made a pass because he'd been unable to resist her! No wonder he'd been able to switch off. He'd been working to a hidden agenda!

'Verity,' he assured her gravely, 'slap and tickle is not my style. It was not my intention to half-seduce you.' His mouth curved wickedly, shooting her nerves into spasm. 'It is not my habit to do anything by halves,' he growled sexily.

'That makes it worse!' she cried heatedly. 'You would have made love to me—'

'Oh, yes,' he murmured with alarming enthusiasm.

'And then,' she began shakily, trembling from a thousand spears of sheer lust, 'I—I suppose you thought I'd be so grateful, so stunned by your expertise, that I'd lie adoring at your feet and be pliant to your every demand!'

He smiled, amused. 'That has a certain appeal, I admit,' he admitted.

'You're impossible!' she yelled, leaping to her feet.

'Honest,' he corrected. 'Verity, can you think about this

rationally for a moment? The car will be here in an hour as I said, and—'

'An hour! You didn't give yourself long! What did you estimate for your seduction time?' she cried indignantly. 'Ten minutes for sex and ten more to spring your surprise on me? Would you have checked your watch and told me to hurry up and climax because the car was almost due?'

He laughed out loud, his teeth white, his smile infuriatingly compelling.

'To be truthful, I was taken by surprise at what happened. Originally, I was just going to put the idea to you. Then I found myself touching you and…' His hands expressed helplessness.

'Oh, sure. You couldn't help what happened!' she finished for him. 'What rubbish! You're a grown man, in charge of your actions—'

'Not entirely. Since meeting you I have been swept along by fate,' he confessed with a wry and charming smile.

She knew what he meant. Maybe he gave in to his urges too often and too easily, but she hadn't been in control of herself, either.

Several times in the past week they'd accidentally touched, or had brushed past one another. Or had found their gazes locked together.

And on those occasions she'd found herself incapable of sensible thought, her mind and body weak as they received the full force of his devastating appeal.

She and goodness knew how many others, she reminded herself tartly. All now forgotten, just a blur of bodies and pleasure. Huh!

'I wish you had let it sweep you somewhere else,' she muttered.

'Well, it didn't. I made a pass and you responded with more enthusiasm than I expected,' he replied baldly.

Flames of shame roared over her skin. So she'd been

eager. But he wasn't much of a gentleman to point that out to her!

'Sorry if my eagerness almost ruined your tightly worked-out schedule!' she snapped, as tart as a lemon.

'I wasn't exactly thinking of it at the time. I couldn't have stopped what happened any more than you could,' he murmured.

Another insult. 'That's where you're wrong. I *did* stop!' she stormed.

'Mmm.' He studied her thoughtfully. 'I'm still not absolutely sure why.'

'I told you. Suddenly I came to my senses!' she raged. 'I realised you disgust me!'

'Really.'

'Yes, really! Maybe it's hard for you to believe,' she spat, 'but I don't like to play around with pleasure-seeking Italian men who wouldn't know a moral if it leapt up and savaged their ankles to rags!'

Infuriatingly, he grinned, as if vastly amused by her unusual turn of phrase.

'I made a mistake then,' he conceded gravely. 'I misread the signs you were giving out.'

She scowled, knowing full well that he'd read them with plumbline accuracy.

'You caught me at a weak moment,' she defended. 'I was tired. Lulled by the meal and the warmth of the wine. I don't like you, Vittore. I loathe shallow men who use women purely for their own needs and then discard them like...like...used light bulbs!' she cried, failing to find a suitable example in her fury.

'Light bulbs?' He was openly laughing at her now.

Verity flushed crossly and hoisted up a wayward shoulder strap, stubbornly searching for a means to defend her choice of words.

'Yes! They get switched on and off whenever you want and then when they're used up, you dump them!'

'Ah. Were you switched on, then?' he teased, his eyes hot and burning.

She had to look away or be desperate for him all over again. How could she deny how she'd felt? She could have lit up a football field all on her own and had enough left over for a small town.

'You're ridiculously vain!' she scorned, ducking the reply. 'And you can forget your so-called solution—'

'Because you think badly of me,' he said soberly, his hands eloquent with regret.

'Understatement,' she clipped.

'But all your information has come from Linda. None of it is from first-hand knowledge.'

'I know that you tried to seduce me—'

'Yes. Why not? You are beautiful and fascinating and wonderful to be with. We have lived intimately for a week and I'm not made of stone. But it doesn't mean I seduce every woman I meet and treat sex casually, or that I was unfaithful during my marriage.'

'But you were unfaithful. Linda said so!' she cried.

'Hmm. Don't you think that she might have lied about my fidelity?' he persisted. 'Think about her for a minute. The kind of person she was. You tell me. Did she ever tell lies when you were children together?'

Verity frowned. All the time, was the answer.

'She might have,' she mumbled grudgingly.

That didn't seem to surprise him at all. And he swept on, 'Would you say she was basically kind, or spiteful? Balanced or hot-tempered?'

He was driving her into a corner. 'I refuse to say anything bad about her. She's dead,' Verity said frostily.

'I admire your sense of honour. But I think, if you're honest, you will have doubts now. Remember that she deliberately spirited my son away and kept me from him. Remember that she lied when she told you that I was dead. If she lied about that, isn't it possible that she told other lies, too? Maybe I am a womaniser, maybe not. You only have the word of a habitual liar for that. And do you honestly think I was a bad father?'

'You have a demanding business. It must take you away from home a lot,' she muttered, the doubts crowding in on her.

'But you can't be sure. I could be innocent. The injured party. I might have cherished my son and spent every free second with him. Why don't you give me the chance to prove she was wrong, and that I can care for Lio?'

'Because I can't take risks with his sanity!' she cried hotly. 'How do I know what you'll do if I go to Italy with you? You could ban me from seeing him, use Italian law to turn me out of your house—'

'Then I'd never gain Lio's love, would I?' he broke in, his tone quiet and measured. 'I'm not such a fool, Verity. I know you are the key to his happiness at the moment. Come with us. Discover what kind of man I am—'

'No!' She shrank back, all too afraid of the man he was—and that she'd discovered far too much already. His presence was overwhelming, his sexual power all too easily capturing her and making her an unwilling victim. 'I can't leave England!' she cried frantically, clinging on to safety. 'It's my home! All my friends are here. And this is where I work, where my contacts are—'

'I'll speak to your employer—' he began evenly.

'I don't have one! I'm self-employed!'

'Then there's no problem,' he reasoned.

'There is,' she scowled, fast running out of objections. 'I'll lose all the goodwill I've built up. I'm staying here.'

'But Lio,' he said softly, 'will be in Italy.'

'Over my dead body!' she cried hotly.

'I don't think I'd have to go *that* far. Just far enough to get what I want.'

She blanched. Took a step back. He'd meant what he'd said. He wouldn't let her stand in his way. She began to tremble.

Vittore stood up and tucked in his shirt, his mocking

eyes observing her horror when she realised that she'd ripped it from his waistband, that she had run her hands over his gloriously muscular chest and had been more intimate with him than any man on earth.

'Don't do this!' she whispered, her mouth dry, her lips so parched they could barely form the words.

'I refuse to continue to go on as we are in this house. If you won't pack Lio's things, then I will,' he announced grimly.

'You won't know what to pack, what he needs!'

'Then help me!'

She stared at him helplessly. 'I'm his guardian! I decide what happens to him! If you try to take him, I'll call the police!' she said shakily.

He gave one of his characteristic shrugs. 'Do that. I have Lio's birth certificate, Linda's death certificate which you kindly handed over to me, and my ID card. I also have Lio's passport. I don't think the police will stop me, as his legal parent, do you? He is morally mine. And if you make a fuss, then I'll get the Press involved. How does this sound? "Spinster aunt denies grieving father his son." Your life would be hell, Verity. As mine has been.'

'You wouldn't!' she breathed.

'I'd do *anything*,' he said, frighteningly quiet, spine-chilling in his determination.

'You *are* a barbarian!' she gasped.

'No.' His black eyes gleamed. 'I am inviting you to come with me. It's you who are thinking of breaking Lio's heart by refusing to accompany him. Choose, Verity. Stay here alone—and have the house sold from under your feet—or come to Italy with me and Lio. Think of it as an all-expenses-paid holiday in a luxury home. To form a relationship with my son I must have you around. I will buy your time. I need you. He needs me. He needs a man in his life as well as a woman.' He smiled. 'How are your football skills?'

'Try me!' she muttered, hoping he wouldn't ask her about the off-side rule.

He gave a lazy smile. 'I will, when we are in Italy.' There was a long and significant pause during which her heart bumped jerkily against her ribs and she wondered just what he meant to try. 'And once Lio and I are totally at ease with one another,' he said with breathtaking simplicity, 'you can return to your friends and the country of your birth.'

Her throat dried again. Quite cold-bloodedly, he was intending to amuse himself with her while she was in Italy and then stick her on a plane when she'd fulfilled her purpose! She couldn't believe his nerve.

'What do I get out of this?' she enquired, her eyes hostile.

'Time with Lio. A pampered existence. Perhaps…me.'

'I knew there was a catch,' she muttered.

Vittore grinned. 'In any case, you will take back with you enough money to set yourself up in business.' He started to walk away. 'Your choice entirely.' He threw her a wicked, mocking glance. 'I'm putting no pressure on you to say "yes".'

'Pressure?' she yelled, striding forwards to confront him. 'I have *no* choice! You know that! You evil, devious brute, you're making me leave everything I love—'

'Apart from Lio,' he pointed out infuriatingly. 'And it would be only temporary. You'll return alone in a couple of months or so to your beloved England.'

Her mouth pruned in. He was wrong. As he'd find out. Lio would never settle. And her nephew would have been dragged away from everything he knew for no benefit at all. The poor kiddie would be in an even worse emotional mess than he was at present. Utterly frustrated, she jammed her fists into her hips as she let off steam.

'It's a terrible risk, uprooting him! And Lio will need me for some time to come! He needs my love—'

'And mine. Can you deny me that, Verity? Can you deny him?'

She chewed at her lip. 'No,' she mumbled. 'But would he get it? You have that business of yours to run. What then? You'd win his confidence and then promptly swan off to your business meetings. Do you think he'll be happy to transfer his affection to a nanny when you leave each day? And can you guarantee that a nanny will love him as I would, and that she'd stay with him till he was old enough not to need her any longer?'

'No,' he said shortly, his face taut with sudden anxiety.

'Now you see the responsibility you're taking on!' she declared heatedly. 'This is a disturbed child we're talking about, Vittore! If you're going to be an absentee father then you might as well leave him here with me! With you, he'd have no stability. You travel the world, I imagine?'

'Yes,' he clipped.

'So there'd be long periods without you at all. Just him and some frequently changing, substitute mother-figure—'

'I'd take him with me!'

'Around the world? To meetings? I don't think so. And if you did, you'd end up employing a nanny or use some hotel baby-sitting service. Or get your current mistress to oblige. In any case, you'd disrupt his routine even more. Lio needs routine. He needs security! Your solution is not good enough!' she declared fiercely.

'Then I'll stay home. Rearrange my affairs—'

'You'd soon get bored. I won't let you do this to Lio! It might give you a kick to be a father, but you're not going to sell the family firm to stay at home with your son, are you? I can't see you abandoning your career for him!'

He frowned, his elegant black brows meeting fiercely together. 'All I know is that he needs to get away from here. I am convinced that this house is half the problem. He watches open doorways anxiously. Jumps when there's an unexplained noise—'

'Then I'll move—'

'Yes. To Italy! He needs to be taken away from the memories that he associates with the house. Verity, I'm certain that something happened here. Perhaps he was left alone or felt frightened of someone or something,' he said firmly. 'We'll probably never know. But he's coming with me tonight and time's running out and I'm not standing here arguing with you. If you won't join us, then that's your decision. I need to move fast if I'm to complete the journey while Lio is asleep.'

'How can you be so stubborn?' she cried helplessly.

'Because I know I am right,' he said, grim and unnervingly determined. 'My son is small and too thin and his speech is non-existent for a child of his age. I can't stand by and watch him suffer. I mean to take him home, where he'll be loved and safe, and where he can grow up normally.'

'You're really taking him, then?' she whispered, aghast.

'Yes.'

She felt sickness clawing at her insides. For Lio's sake she had to go along with this stupid plan.

'You don't care about his needs,' she accused bitterly. 'You're just satisfying your own selfish wants—'

'You'll come?' he barked.

'You know I have to!' she snapped. 'I don't want to. I don't want Lio uprooted, either. But you know I can't stop you. So go ahead. Force me to live in your wretched house! I suppose I'll have to lock my door every night to stop you taking droit de seign...senn...'

'Squatters' rights?' he suggested, drily amused.

Furious, she raised her hand to hit him but he caught it. They tussled and she was in his arms, her body bent back as she writhed and squirmed helplessly. For a glorious moment his mouth was on hers; fierce, hard, crazily welcome. Her body melded into his and she felt control slipping away from her again.

'You are irresistible,' he murmured, imbuing even those

words with slow, languorous sensuality. 'Verity. Think of the pleasure we'll have together!'

'Go to hell!' she sobbed and, fleeing her own weakness, she ran up the stairs—or rather, fell up them.

He was with her in a moment. 'Here,' he said soothingly, rubbing her shin with gentle fingers.

His eyes silvered. She gave a little whimper as his hand slid further, caressing the back of her knee and then, with heart-stopping slowness, moved up her thigh. Then it was removed. And he must have known that her gasp was one of disappointment.

'I loathe you!' she jerked miserably.

'I like the way you do it,' he countered with a smile.

This time her hand connected in a hard slap, though not with his face. His palm met hers, his fingers entwining like a knot as he stared intently into her eyes.

'I will make love to you,' he promised huskily, and sexual hunger exploded inside her again. 'Sooner or later, you will succumb. I want you, Verity. More than any woman I've ever known.'

His head swooped and she gritted her teeth so the kiss gave him no pleasure. But when he let his mouth soften and coax her lips apart, her senses began to reel.

He was a skilled lover, she thought in despair. And if she didn't keep reminding herself what a shallow Casanova he was, she'd be another notch on his bedpost.

If there was any room left there. In any case, she would lose all self-respect. With a sudden twist, she released herself and stalked on up the stairs, turning to glare at him.

'I'm impressed you can remember all your women to make a comparison,' she said sourly.

He joined her on the landing, casually leaning on the balustrade.

'Every single one,' he assured her in amusement.

And to her dismay, that raised a terrible jealousy within her that scoured the pit of her stomach. Sex, to him, was a game. A male right. And she'd been marked out as his next victim.

All she had to do was to make sure she never let down her guard, never surrendered. All! She groaned inwardly, knowing how hard that would be when her senses clamoured for him.

Stony-faced, she levelled her violet gaze at him and said with glacial contempt, 'I will come with you because I have no choice. But don't expect me to encourage Lio to become fond of you. I don't think that would be in his best interests.'

The dark eyes glittered. 'You'd deliberately turn him against me?'

'No. That would upset him,' she muttered. 'I'm just not doing a PR job for you.'

'I'm relieved to hear it. Verity, I know what I feel about him. I also know what I feel when I am with you,' he murmured.

Marching towards her bedroom, with Vittore close on her heels, she quelled the wicked, treacherous excitement that was trying to ruin her rejection of him, and wished she could find a way to protect herself. If he succeeded in getting her into his bed, then…

Her breath drew in sharply as something awful occurred to her. Was that a deliberate tactic? Did he think that Lio would look more *favourably* on someone she slept with and openly kissed and cuddled?

Her stomach swooped like an express lift as reality set in. Look at her! Unsophisticated, tousled, lacking glamour… She had to be honest. Why would a man like Vittore even glance at her, when he could be trawling the night clubs of Monaco and Paris and New York for svelte, glossy women who knew one end of a Sharutti handbag from another? She couldn't even spell the designer name, let alone afford anything attached to it.

That was it then. He'd imagined the three of them snuggling up on the sofa like a happy family. And once he had Lio's confidence, she'd be for the chop.

Huh! She'd never let him near her, she thought darkly. She paused by her bedroom door. Vittore was so confident that his scheme would work... She gave a small, triumphant smile. She'd use that arrogance to her advantage.

'Very well.'

'You'll come?'

She turned, found him disconcertingly close. Her eyes warned him to back off and he did so. She had the impression that he was waiting anxiously for her answer and that gave her a small advantage.

'Yes, I'll come, without argument or complaint. But I have one condition,' she declared calmly, pleased with her brainwave.

He gave an expansive wave of his hand. 'Name it.'

Got him! she thought. Now she had a chance to become the legitimate guardian of Lio, to give him the attention he craved—and to bring him up to be honest and decent and to respect women.

There was something so innocent and untouched about a small child, and she shuddered to think of Vittore's dreadful morals gradually perverting her nephew. She owed this to Linda. She'd been given a responsibility and she intended to guard her nephew from any bad influence.

'Right. It's this. You must win Lio's confidence in the next six months. Otherwise you must admit defeat and let me bring him back to England,' she stated boldly. 'You can visit him, of course,' she added as an afterthought.

'Agreed,' he said, supremely self-assured, just as she'd hoped. 'You have my word.' He grinned, a teasing light making his eyes sparkle.

'Shake on it,' she ordered.

'With pleasure.'

'It will be!' she promised grimly.

With an eyebrow arching in query, his hand clasped hers. The light bulb effect lasted for the few, tingling seconds that their hands were joined and then he slowly withdrew his fingers, letting them trail tantalisingly across her palm to her trembling fingertips.

'You're very sure of yourself, aren't you?' he mused.

'Positive. We've seen how he's been this past week. You've made no progress. Lio needs me,' she said firmly. 'Linda wanted him to be in my care, not yours. I intend to fulfil her wishes.'

'What about a bet on your chances?' he murmured.

She gave him a scornful glance. 'I don't have any money to bet.'

'But you do have *something* I want.'

The breath left her lungs. She swallowed and her hands found the reassuring solidity of her bedroom door.

'Oh?' she said, as if she didn't know. She trawled around for a witty remark but her brain had become filled with fog.

'Prove how sure you are,' he goaded. 'Take my bet—'

'If it involves playing nanny and playboy with you, forget it!' she scathed.

He smiled and she had the distinct feeling that she was a fly, about to fall into his web.

'This is a more interesting version,' he drawled. 'You see, I am convinced that Lio will soon become comfortable with me, and that he will be happy to stay with me even when you're not around.'

'You are so wrong!' she retorted scornfully.

'Then you'll have no hesitation in agreeing to my suggestion,' he said with wide-eyed innocence.

But she knew Vittore's innocence had been lost a long time ago. 'Which is?' she said, assuming a bored expression.

'Very simple. If I win Lio's confidence *before* the next six months are up, then you will come willingly to my bed and we will be lovers until I have had enough of you.'

Her jaw dropped in amazement and now the door met

her spine as she slumped against it, the wind taken from her lungs.

'I can't believe you just said that!' she croaked. 'It's *outrageous*—!'

'Yes.' His hands came either side of her shoulders, trapping her. His dark eyes gazed down inscrutably. 'But you are so sure it will never happen, so…'

Wide-eyed, she stared at his sensual mouth, parted as if for a kiss, the teeth pearly white, lips arched and inviting…

Suddenly she was overwhelmed by a multitude of shocking whispers ricocheting around inside her head. She cringed back against the door, trying to keep a space between the two of them.

Unbelievably, her body and her brain were excited by his challenge. It was as if she wanted him to win. But of course, he wouldn't. No problem, then—she would be safe. A virgin still.

A twinge of disappointment scurried its wicked way through her, shaming and thrilling her in equal measures. Any excuse, it seemed, and she'd let him bed her!

It was because she'd never had a megawatt man interested in her before and had never felt so horribly out of control as she did whenever he turned his power-station electrics in her direction.

She'd get used to it in time. She wanted to be a woman in a million—a billion, even!—and not one who'd be bedded and forgotten in a few months by the biggest love rat in Europe.

Until he'd had enough of her, indeed!

He was looking at her with such smug amusement that she wanted to shock him, wanted to call his bluff and show he was wrong. She would be the one that got away.

She'd prove to him that not all women succumbed to a handsome face, a hunky body, charisma, money, breeding, good manners and elegant tailoring.

Verity blinked then frowned at the list of his attributes. Too much for any man, she thought crossly. Time he discovered that kindness, honesty and reliability were just as important to some women.

And recklessness got the better of caution and she found herself tossing up her head till her curls bounced, declaring haughtily, 'Fine by me! You haven't a snowball's hope in hell.'

The pool-deep eyes liquefied. She felt the hunger, that surge of nerve-wrecking electricity, forming an irresistible connection between them. Her body almost swayed towards him helplessly.

This was madness, she thought in panic. What was she agreeing to?

'Then you have nothing to worry about, have you?' he murmured, his lashes making achingly beautiful black crescents on his cheeks as he stared entranced at her softly parted mouth.

She shut it tightly and pinched it in. Now she didn't feel so sure of herself. He'd said he'd do anything...

'No dirty tricks,' she warned him coldly, pressed as flat against the door as any curvy body could be.

Warmth flowed from him: warm body, warm breath, warm eyes. She did her best to stay frosted even while her limbs turned to meltwater.

And he was doing that innocent look again. 'Like what?'

She had to think back for a moment, plundering her memory banks for her last remark. Yes. Dirty tricks.

'I don't know!' she snapped, wishing he'd ease up on the close body contact. 'Plying Lio with chocolate and ice-cream to bribe him. Locking me up so he has to bond with you. Spiking my drink so I can't defend myself when you pounce—'

'I'm not a pouncer,' he said in amusement. 'Allow me a little more finesse than that.'

It wasn't funny. She glared. 'Everything above board. Promise,' she insisted.

'I promise,' he said solemnly. 'No injections of love-potions at dead of night, no rose petals on your pillow or vodka in your tea—'

'There's no need to make fun!' she said crossly, quite liking the idea of rose petals on her pillow. 'You could get up to anything, and I have to protect Lio and myself.'

'And I admire your touching concern for him,' he replied quietly. The corners of his mouth lifted in a slow smile. 'Even while I find your suggestions highly amusing. I'm looking forward to the time we spend together, Verity. I find the prospect…exciting.'

So did she. And worrying, too. She sighed. It was all so confusing. Had she thought of everything? No… Her face clouded.

'There's one big problem, Vittore,' she said, her eyes pastel with anxiety. 'If Lio is clearly desperately upset in Italy, *before* the six months are up, what then?'

He winced and pulled away, freeing her from his claustrophobic presence. She could breathe freely at last, instead of taking little gulps of air and fighting to get them down to her starving lungs.

'What then, Vittore?' she demanded, more in control of herself.

'In that case, you must take him back to England,' he said huskily. 'I wouldn't want to put him through hell. Nor could I bear to watch him suffer. All I ask is for a little time for him to settle down.' His voice grew quieter and he said in choking tones, 'If he doesn't, I will accept that he will be better off with you.'

He had a few scraps of decency, it seemed and for that she had to be grateful. She shifted uncomfortably, his tense expression oddly painful to her.

'Thank you,' she said grudgingly. 'I'll pack my stuff, then Lio's.'

Extraordinarily, it took a great effort to resist the urge to put a comforting hand on his arm. Who knew where that might lead? But she did feel compassion for him. Losing his son for the second time would be a devastating blow.

'Shake on it.'

Their hands clasped. She shivered at the sudden glow that lit his feral eyes and she fought to break the spell he seemed determined to cast over her.

'I wish you weren't so optimistic. You ought to prepare yourself for failure,' she warned.

The smile that played around Vittore's lips was worryingly confident and made her heart skip a beat.

'I won't fail. You see, Verity, there is no such word in my vocabulary,' he informed her.

'May I remind you of the colours that ran in the washing machine?' she countered sarkily.

'That wasn't failure. Just lack of information,' he excused with an airy wave of his hand. 'When I have time with Lio in my own home, he and I will become very close.'

'Not a chance,' she retorted firmly, and strode off to pack.

But despite her bravado she was scared. Although he'd promised no dirty tricks, she wondered fearfully what he had in store for her. She was going into the unknown. And taking an innocent child there, too.

CHAPTER SIX

FOR the first part of the journey she hardly spoke, feeling so angry with Vittore for treating her like a commodity that she could barely bring herself to do more than scowl. But that was tiring after a while, and it wasn't in her nature to sulk.

Besides, whether she liked it or not, she felt very cherished. She had to admit that Vittore could be very attentive. And, she reflected, his wealth had made the trip smooth and easy. No wonder Linda had been addicted to being pampered and had tried to keep up her previous lifestyle.

A hired chauffeur had stowed their luggage and fussed the three of them into the back of the limousine, offering tea, coffee and canapés to amuse them on the journey to the airport. Verity had sampled everything as a matter of principle.

They'd swept through customs without any effort, a porter carrying the sleeping Lio as if he were transporting beaten gold. Which he virtually was, of course.

For the very rich, it seemed there were no queues, no hold-ups, no two-hour check-ins. The jet had been waiting on the tarmac and took off once they were comfortably settled with magazines, papers and telephones.

She used one of the latter to call her close friends. All fourteen of them. Vittore didn't seem bothered at all and she supposed the price of fourteen lengthy phone calls was a drop in the ocean to him.

Sitting in opulent comfort on Vittore's private jet, Verity sighed and nibbled a hand-made chocolate. Lemon cream. Her favourite. She sighed. A girl could get used to such luxuries.

And she might as well make the most of them. Lio would make his feelings clear and she'd be back in England with him soon, heaving the buggy on buses again and tramping the streets comparing the price of bread.

'Brandy?' murmured the steward, with a delightful smile.

'Thank you…' Smiling at the steward, she returned to her final call. 'No, Sue. I'll be fine. I'll send you a post-card… What was that? Oh, *him*!' She flushed as if her friend had sussed out her secret feelings for her brother-in-law. 'The words ''arrogant'' and ''egocentric'' spring to mind,' she reported scathingly. The pink Italian newspaper, which Vittore was reading, rustled with annoyance. Verity smiled with satisfaction and answered Sue's next question. 'Nothing to write home about. Horribly unshaven at the moment. Tall, dark, wears suits,' she dismissed, trying not to think of the way those suits flattered the hunky body beneath. 'Sure. When we return. Lunch will be great. I'll do scrambled egg on toast. OK? See you. Bye.'

Rakishly handsome with his designer stubble, Vittore peered out from the newspaper, his expression cynical.

'When Lio wakes he'll need your undivided attention,' he drawled. 'I suggest you sleep while you can. There's a bed in the inner cabin.'

She cut him with a glance. 'No thanks. I don't want to become a member of the mile high club,' she said coldly.

He laughed. 'You will,' he promised. 'Give me time.'

And he resumed reading his paper while Verity glared, unnoticed, at the pink sheets covered in columns of figures till she realised that Lio was stirring. He moaned, his eyes opening wide.

Silently Vittore lay down his paper, watching her tensely as she sat by Lio's car seat, rhythmically stroking his fore-head.

'Hush,' she whispered. 'Hush. Go to sleep, sweetheart. I'm here.'

She knew Lio fidgeted in his sleep sometimes, and

wasn't really awake. So she sang to him softly till he fell asleep again and she curled up in the reclining seat beside him, making no comment when Vittore draped a blanket over her and switched off the cabin light.

'Verity.'

Her eyes flew open to find him bending over her, his face very close to hers. Automatically she cringed back in the seat. Instantly he moved back, his dark eyes veiled.

'This is not an attack on your virtue,' he said drily. 'You've been asleep. Time to wake up. We're coming in to land.'

He snapped her up into the upright position and as she muzzily fumbled for the seat belt she found that he was already fastening it. He must have washed and shaved, because she caught a drift of expensive cologne, and his jaw was smooth and satiny.

Trickles of pleasure curled through her veins. And her pulses went crazy when he dropped a kiss on her sleepy mouth. As he drew back, the suppressed joy in his face silenced her protest.

'Forgive me. I couldn't resist it. I'm bursting with happiness!' he whispered.

'Well, burst over someone else,' she muttered.

'I would,' he countered, 'but there's only the pilot or the steward apart from you and they'd sue me if I kissed them.'

'I wouldn't bet on it. They both looked gaga when you grinned at them,' she grumbled, and he laughed.

Vittore was still chuckling when he leant over to check that Lio was safely secured. And as he gazed at his son, back came the look of sheer radiant joy that once again caught at Verity's heart.

'Nearly home, Lio,' he said in choked tones.

Then he turned as if to hide his face from her and with his eyes resolutely cast down, he fixed his own seat belt.

She felt shaken by his fervour. It occurred to her that he

was so eager to reclaim his son that he might try to rush things with Lio. She would need to monitor Vittore very carefully. She braced herself for a bumpy ride.

Their arrival, of course, was beautifully smooth. An official met them on the tarmac, gave a cursory glance at their documents and waved them on, even pausing to admire the oblivious Lio, and to help Vittore clip the baby seat into the back of the waiting Mercedes.

Verity found herself trembling. Lio's happiness was her responsibility. And now they were in Italy, she might have a battle royal on her hands with Vittore. All her self-confidence ebbed away. Here she was reliant on him for everything: a roof over her head, food, interpreting the language…

'Do we have a long way to go?' she asked in a subdued tone, as he cheerfully started the car.

'Not far in actual distance, though it'll take a while because of the twisting mountain roads. At the moment we're in Napoli.'

'Naples?' she queried.

'That's right. We're driving to the coast, near Amalfi.' His voice softened noticeably. 'It is very beautiful there, Verity. I think you will appreciate it. And life will be much easier for you because my staff will do everything for us so you can concentrate on Lio.'

'He won't like people lurking about!' she protested.

'They'll keep a low profile till Lio is settled,' Vittore assured her. 'You have my word on that. Dishes will be washed, meals cooked, beds made—and you'll never see those people responsible.'

It was like a fairy tale. All the domestic chores done as if by magic. Very appealing!

But she fell silent, wondering how she'd cope with living in a billionaire's mansion. Vittore seemed very happy and utterly relaxed. He might well be. He was on his home ground. She, however, felt as if her nerves were jangling like a thousand cracked bells.

At first, once they'd left Naples, they sped along a motorway. She must have slept again because the next time she stared out of the window the road had turned into a corkscrew, that twisted hectically around the edge of a mountain. Sheer drops were on one side and brutal rock on the other, both dramatic options picked out starkly by the car's powerful headlights.

The stars hung above them, more brilliant than she'd ever known, the Milky Way a beautiful mist across the velvety sky. Occasionally a light would flicker from a remote building and she wondered who would be up and awake at this early hour in the morning. A farmer perhaps, or a mother tending to a fretful baby.

'You won't let anyone keep me from Lio, will you?' she asked, suddenly afraid of Vittore's intentions. 'And you'll let me manage him in my own way?'

'I care about him,' he answered gravely. 'That's why you're here—because he needs you. You have to trust me on this.'

'I can't,' she said miserably.

'I know. But you will. Try to relax and only bite me if I bite you.'

'Not likely! I'd get the plague,' she muttered.

Vittore grinned with delight. 'What a woman!' he marvelled and she made a note not to be so smart.

'I think I can see the sea,' she claimed, adroitly changing the subject.

'You're right,' he said, his voice husky and loving. 'The Divine Coast.'

In the glimmer of the first dawn light, she saw umbrella pines, silhouetted against a grey mass that moved and shimmered with soft lights. As they drove along, the greyness turned first gold then became a rose pink sea as the dawn rolled back the darkness and heralded a new day.

Verity could now make out rolling hills covered in pinewoods and olive trees. And they were driving along a vicious, tortuous road hacked out of solid rock which flung them in one direction and then another as they sped around dozens of hairpin bends.

'Oh, my life!'

Startled, she gripped the edge of her seat as they swung out, seemingly towards the edge of a precipitous cliff with the sea far below.

'You're not too nervous? It's perfectly safe if you know what you're doing, and I'm driving very carefully. I have a precious cargo on board,' he assured her gently.

She blinked, surprised to find that she felt excited, and turned bright eyes on Vittore, totally captivated by the breathtaking view. Divine indeed. The coast. His enraptured face.

She bit her lip and found a scrap of common sense from somewhere. 'The road doesn't worry me. It's just breathtaking. I've never seen anywhere more beautiful!' she exclaimed in awe.

'The bluest sea in the world. The most stunning scenery,' he said happily. 'I'd stop for us to admire it, but I want to get home before Lio wakes.'

His voice had shaken. Verity's heart lurched. 'This must mean a great deal to you,' she said quietly, thinking of the return journey when Vittore would be sending his child back to England. Something stabbed at her chest, as if shards of glass had impaled themselves in her ribs.

'It means everything. There are no words to express what is in my heart.'

He swallowed and she knew he couldn't say any more. Once again, her own tender heart was being won over. There was a lump in her own throat as she gazed at the sea, which was turning a lapis lazuli before her very eyes.

It was all too seductive, she thought apprehensively. And the happiness that shone in Vittore's face and energised his entire body, was tugging unfairly at her emotions.

She was being swayed by a father's natural love for his son, for the flesh and blood tie that bound them. And it was hard to hold on to the fact that Linda had not wanted

Vittore to take care of Lio. She had to discover the reason. She must.

In the meantime, she turned her attention to a tumble of houses ahead which seemed to be cascading down to the sea. In the harbour, brightly coloured boats bobbed on the azure water and others were drawn up on the sandy cove.

Enchanted, she wound the window down and caught the tang of salt on the breeze and the heady perfume from the orange trees which clung perilously to the slopes. She inhaled and finally relaxed, dazed by the beauty of it all as a bell began to toll, echoing out across the peach-coloured buildings.

Too perfect, she thought, her heart hammering loudly. Too alluring.

'This is San Lorenzo,' Vittore said huskily and she felt that he was seeing it with different eyes because he was bringing his beloved son back home. 'I live just beyond the town.'

'It looks impossibly picturesque,' she observed, wishing she didn't find it quite so appealing.

'That's because it has evolved naturally over the centuries,' he replied lovingly. 'We have an eye for beauty.' He smiled at her then flicked his eyes back to the road. 'There were only mule tracks until relatively recently. Access was mainly from the sea, so the town's defences are concentrated there. Look, you can see one of the gates and the line of the medieval walls.'

'You'd need powerful thigh muscles and a touch of madness to mount an attack up that steep slope,' she mused.

Vittore smiled. 'I think the Saracen pirates were tough enough for the challenge.'

He shifted his leg and she found herself staring at the outline of his thigh beneath the fine linen. She'd had some experience of his strength. If he wanted, he could overpower her.

Once he'd said that he was very controlled except when

his passions were engaged. And...his passion was considerable. Had he...? No. It was unthinkable that he would have forced Linda against her will. Vittore had a gentle side, a tenderness that she'd admired.

And also a fiery passion.

The question nagged in her mind as they drove slowly through a huge stone arch and into canyons of narrow streets. She felt a flicker of panic. Linda had fled this Paradise. And she badly needed to find out why.

'Cold?' he asked, lightly touching the goosebumps on her arms.

She jammed her finger on the button beside her and closed the window, jerking her arm and its goosebumps away and pretending the heat in her loins didn't exist.

'Bit fresh,' she said meaningfully.

He chuckled and suddenly they were out of the narrow streets and in a pretty little piazza. Vittore pointed out the Chiesa San Lorenzo, the local church, and its thirteenth-century tower whose sonorous bell she'd heard earlier.

In the small street leading from the piazza she spotted bijou jewellers, a chocolate shop and an elegant store apparently selling nothing but silk.

'I thought it would be quaint and olde worlde, not full of exclusive boutiques,' she exclaimed in surprise, turning this way and that.

'Italians are earthy and passionate and have a love for beautiful things. Food, buildings, clothes...women.'

She ignored that, though the apparent contradictions intrigued her. 'Earthy and sophisticated,' she mused.

'The town is a shopaholic's delight. There's a baby boutique to the left, and several famous designer outlets you'd like,' Vittore agreed rather cynically, seeing how she seemed fascinated by the shops.

'Designers? Me? They'd have a fit if I wandered in wearing one of my second-hand outfits!' she declared. 'I don't shop in the normal sense. I just press my nose against windows and look wistful till someone offers me a penny to go away,' she joked. Vittore laughed and she felt stupidly pleased. 'My budget doesn't stretch to luxuries,' she added, bringing herself back to earth.

Or even essentials, she thought, suddenly alarmed at the potential expense of living in such a glamorous location. Frantically she scrabbled in her purse. The few small denomination notes in there looked lonely.

'I—I'll have to change some money,' she continued. 'I don't have much because I spent my savings on things for Lio—'

'Please.'

His hand briefly touched her thigh, drying her mouth immediately so she couldn't speak without betraying herself. And causing her body to tense up and set off all kinds of reactions in some highly personal regions.

Why did it do that? she thought crossly. Why couldn't she be immune to his wretched hand? It was just flesh and blood and bone—and yet it had the power to heat her up like an oven turned up to Gas Mark 5.

'I wish you wouldn't touch me!' she complained, producing a weird, gravelly voice. She hoped she'd sounded cross, rather than husky.

'I'm sorry. It was to reassure you,' he told her smoothly. 'I don't want you to worry about money. You have protected Lio over these past weeks and unselfishly changed your life for his sake. I know it must have been hard to do this all on your own, with no previous experience. I want to express my thanks in practical terms. You'll be well paid while you're here. And if you refuse to accept my money,' he said with a grin, 'then I'll bundle you back on the plane. Your services are of great value, Verity. I don't expect to get them for nothing.'

She looked surprised. 'But I can't—!'

His hand melted into her thigh again. She found her body soaring up to oven temperature again.

'No buts,' he insisted. 'I owe you a debt that can never

be properly paid. Don't put me further in your debt. Allow me to pay you a salary.'

She sat there, sizzling, and tried to think rationally. Yes, she was out of pocket. She did need some essentials. And if he saw her as an employee, then their relationship might become more formal.

Nanny and employer.

Her mouth curved into an amused smile. Still in her old cotton dress the colour of violets, its slightly shrunken shape clinging from bosom to ankle, and with her hair tousled into gypsy curls by the wind, she was the least likely nanny anyone could imagine!

'OK. I'll accept your offer—so long as I don't have to call you "sir". Thank you,' she said, unable to suppress a giggle.

'Joke?' he murmured.

'Oh, only that I'm not nanny material. Your mother will have a fit.'

His teeth flashed white in his olive-skinned face.

'Don't be too sure. Wait till you meet her!' he said, in tones of amused despair.

'Why? Is she awful?' Verity laughed.

'Wonderful,' he replied. 'But nothing like a mother. You, however, have all the qualities a woman and mother should possess.'

'Italians exaggerate horribly,' she countered, rather appalled by her pleasure at his flattery. She knew he was flirting, that silken compliments came naturally to him, but she wanted to hear them, nevertheless. How stupid of her. How weak and desperate!

'We do exaggerate,' he admitted, immediately reducing her ego to a manageable size. 'It adds pleasure to life and makes people feel good about themselves. But in your case I mean what I say.'

He might as well know the truth, she thought with a sigh.

'I'm untidy, unorthodox and stubborn. I can't make

cakes the shape of cute bunnies or steam trains, would prefer to be gardening rather than ironing and the thought of talking with other mothers about potty training fills me with horror.'

'Exactly. As I said. Perfect.'

Surreptitiously, Verity stole a glance at him. His face had softened and become heart-achingly tender. When he'd spoken, it had been with great sincerity and the low-pitched sound of his voice had seeped beguilingly into every treacherously eager cell of her body.

She sniffed indignantly. He was definitely trying to seduce her. And making a very good job of it, if her stratospheric pulse rate was any guide.

'Stop trying so hard to charm me,' she said caustically. 'It won't work.'

'Who's trying?' His hands described his innocence. 'I'm stating facts. You are unusually beautiful, warm, passionate and caring. You have a directness, a wonderful sense of humour and a disconcerting honesty. I feel I can trust you. And I have found it impossible to trust any woman—other than those I've known all my life—since Linda took Lio away.'

She frowned, glowing from the rather unreal picture he'd painted of her.

'I'd like to know what happened between you two,' she said quietly.

In an instant his face grew dark. 'I don't want to talk about it.'

Verity gave a sigh of exasperation. 'You said you wanted me to discover what kind of man you are. How can I, if—?'

'By observation. Not gossip,' he said shortly.

'Vittore, it won't be gossip if you tell me—'

'No!' he muttered. 'It's in the past. Forget it.'

But she knew she couldn't. A question mark hung over him and his behaviour. And until she learned the truth, she'd never trust him.

His mood had changed. He brooded, his eyes fierce beneath lowered brows, his mouth drawn into a tight, uncompromising line.

'That's my house.'

Curt and formal, he nodded towards a large and elegant building above the sea, its terraced grounds running down to a sandy beach.

'House? Good grief! More like a palace!' she exclaimed, sitting forwards uncertainly.

'It was.' He seemed remote from her, his joy evaporated as he said in clipped tones, 'The *Palazzo di Fiorenzi*. The palace of the Florentine princes. They built it in the eighteenth century as a winter retreat.'

Verity fell silent, oddly disturbed by his coldness and stunned by the grandeur of his *palazzo*. She reflected that he'd brought Linda here as a bride. Her adoptive sister had had everything wealth could buy and yet she had run from it.

She shivered, even more afraid of what he'd done to drive the luxury-loving, materialistic Linda from a life of unparalleled comfort.

Apprehensively she watched a pair of huge iron gates swing open at a flick of Vittore's remote controller, and then she turned around fearfully as the gates closed with a loud clang.

Now she was a virtual prisoner, she thought, her heart beginning to pound.

'Will I have one of those?' she asked nervously, indicating the controller.

'If you drive. Otherwise you'll use the *citofono*—the entry phone.'

'So I'll be able to go out if I want?' she asked doubtfully.

'If someone is with you.'

'Am I that dangerous to the local population?' she quipped, in an effort to cover up her nerves.

'You might run off with Lio and I'd never see him again.'

Verity gasped. 'I'd never do that to you!'

'Your sister did.'

'Adoptive sister. And what she did has no connection with me.' She glanced at him warily. 'So you mean to keep me locked up and treat me like a criminal!'

He shot her a frowning look. 'You can do what you like, providing you're escorted. I wouldn't make you a prisoner. What kind of man do you think I am?' he asked.

'I don't know!' she muttered. 'I wish I did!'

'Then the sooner you find out the better,' he said grimly. 'I'll show you around properly later. Let's just get in and take Lio to the nursery before the staff—and he—awake.'

'They must be careful not to scare him—'

'They know about his problem. I called them from the plane. Here we are. Welcome to my home,' he said formally, as if remembering his manners. '*Daverro*, it's good to be back!' he continued under his breath. 'To be here, with my son…'

She was too stunned to make any coherent response or comment. Her astonished eyes were scanning the gorgeous gardens, tumbling with flowers and exotic foliage. Huge paddle-shaped leaves of banana plants soared above towering ginger and canna plants. Tall oleander trees jostled with palms and mimosa trees.

And amazingly, great mounds of climbing roses had been allowed to heap themselves up, like breakers tumbling to the shore. A riot of colour dazzled the eye and delighted butterflies danced over the haze of flowers.

'This is like no Italian garden I've ever seen in my garden books!' she declared. 'They're usually on geometric lines, with neat box hedges and stone statues of nudes, and cypress trees like exclamation marks,' she said in awe, itching to explore the garden more closely.

'My mother's doing,' Vittore grumped. 'She doesn't like manicured or formal gardens.'

Verity cheered up, feeling she might have a kindred spirit to talk to.

'I think I might like your mother.'

'She'll be here later. After *Lo struscio*.'

'The what?'

He gave a little 'tut' of irritation, as if talking to her was a burden.

'It means "strutting your stuff". The evening stroll where you wander up and down staring at everyone else and seeing what they're wearing and who they're with.'

'Your mother struts her stuff?' Verity said in amazement, warming even more to the woman.

While she absorbed that, he drew up at the foot of a double flight of marble steps which led to an imposing portico.

Vittore leapt out, his fingers impatiently unstrapping the car seat.

'You'll understand when you see her.'

He lifted the seat as if it weighed nothing and carried Lio inside. All she could do was to follow with Lio's changing bag, her heart beginning to bump about uncomfortably.

They marched across a huge, marbled hall and up a grand staircase lit by an enormous crystal chandelier. On the honey-coloured walls, the subjects of the ancestral portraits stared at her disapprovingly, following her with their oil-dark eyes.

Verity felt very small and humble. This place was too huge, too vast for Lio. He'd hate it. And she'd have to mop up his tears and quieten his screams.

Her heart sank to her boots. It was a lovely house in stunning surroundings but their stay was likely to be short and harrowing. She reckoned they'd be on their way back home after four weeks.

To her astonishment, a deep depression swept over her, leaving her with a sense of impending loss that she couldn't shake off. And, as she followed Vittore along the elegantly furnished landing, she realised to her dismay that he was the root cause of her low spirits.

She wallowed in a rare gloom. She wanted him but knew she must not feed her hunger. It was like wanting forbidden fruit. Fatal but utterly desirable. She was aware of all the reasons why she shouldn't let him get close, but nevertheless she felt an unstoppable desire. And every hour they were together that need grew stronger.

Verity scowled, despising herself for falling into Vittore's trap so easily. He'd make love to her, win Lio over, and send her back home, used and unwanted.

So her best bet would be to mentally tattoo 'Remember, Verity: you are a means to an end' all over her eyeballs and hope that would be enough to remind her that Vittore was a danger to her health—and to Lio's future welfare, too.

'Here's the nursery.' Vittore smiled at her: happy, confident, triumphant.

Her pulses did their usual sprint but she remained outwardly cool and even managed to unclip Lio from the car seat without too much fumbling.

'Just in time. He's stirring,' she observed. 'Incidentally, you'll have to buy something larger than that crib.'

'I know. Haven't had the opportunity yet.' Vittore seemed agitated.

So was she. Lio might yell his head off at the strange surroundings. Carefully she sat on a nursing chair close to the crib, with Lio in her arms.

'You'd better move back out of sight,' she warned Vittore.

'Of course.'

His huskiness reached deep inside her, disturbing her more than she would have liked. It was her kind nature, she told herself. A knee-jerk response to a father's frustrated love. Nothing to do with worrying about Vittore's feelings.

Lio knuckled his eyes and then opened them blearily, his blond hair matted from sleep.

'Hello, sweetheart!' she murmured with a smile.

Grumpily he buried his face in her lap and stuck his bottom in the air. A hand quickly appeared to her right, Vittore's strong, brown fingers setting a mobile in motion, the lambs, cows and pigs bobbing merrily.

The tune sounded sweetly in the quietness of the room and Lio slowly turned over. A beaming smile broke across his face and he laughed, reaching up for the animals. Still waiting for a perturbed yell, Verity lifted him up so that he could see them more clearly, saying the names of each bobbing animal. Lio rewarded her with a huge, dazzling smile that reminded her so forcefully of Vittore's grin that her stomach contracted.

'Come on. You need changing,' she muttered.

She looked around but Vittore had gone. Surprised, she made a hasty recce of the room, found there was an en suite bathroom attached, and decided to pop Lio into the bath. They played happily with the boats and ducks and when he was dry and had been set down, she again waited for him to object to the alien surroundings.

Oddly, he seemed to love them, his little face bright and sunny with pleasure as he eagerly toddled about and explored the toy boxes.

Perhaps Vittore had been right about the need to leave Linda's house, she reflected, when she later dressed Lio by the full-length window. Though any child would be charmed by the hand-painted jungle scenes on the wall and the fascinating toys everywhere.

Someone had obviously bought things unsuitable for the three-month old baby that he had once been, thinking of the future when Lio would be more active. And she knew that person was probably Vittore. Seeing all the unused toys must have been heartbreaking for him, she thought with a pang.

'Hey, wriggly worm, stand still!' she pleaded with Lio,

trying to manoeuvre his T-shirt over his hand while it still clutched a shiny red Maserati.

The shirt popped into place. She tapped his button nose playfully and he laughed, then stared out of the window, his eyes anxious.

Verity followed his gaze. 'It's Papa,' she said softly.

Solemnly the little boy watched his father sitting on the terrace below, sipping a cup of coffee and taking occasional bites from a croissant. Verity waited with baited breath, stilled by the significance of the moment.

Then Lio turned away, his forehead furrowed, lower lip stuck out in dismay.

'It's all right, sweetheart. I'm here, aren't I? Are you hungry?' And of course Lio nodded. He had a good appetite. 'Right. Let's go down. Breakfast!' she said eagerly, taking his small hand in hers.

But she caught a movement on the terrace below and paused. An elderly man—obviously someone on Vittore's staff—had appeared and was talking to Vittore, his face alight with pleasure. To her astonishment, Vittore rose and the two men hugged. The older man had tears in his eyes when they separated and shook hands, pumping one another's arms up and down vigorously. There was no mistaking the man's affection for Vittore.

Lio was tugging her to come away and so she slowly walked down the stairs with him, then, after opening a series of doors and finding no exit to the garden, she suddenly struck lucky, seeing open doors leading to the terrace at the far end of a large, high-ceilinged and frescoed salon.

The period room was imposing, with beautifully upholstered antique settles and deep armchairs and yet it had a homely air, with family belongings everywhere. A sun hat, flung casually on a table. An open book, abandoned on the floor and newspapers stacked on a small ornate table. Someone's silk cardigan draped over the back of a chair. A pair of court shoes abandoned, where someone had obviously kicked them off by the sofa.

And there were dozens and dozens of photographs everywhere. She couldn't stop to examine them properly because Lio was keen to go outside, but she did manage to slow their pace down and scan them quickly.

Most seemed to be of Lio and his father, from Lio's birth to, presumably, when he was three months old. They were natural shots, not set-up poses, many clearly surprising Vittore and taken as he changed his baby's nappy, bathed him, or dressed him. In all of them, Vittore looked happy and adoring, the light in his eyes betraying his deep love for his son.

That gave her cause for thought. The photos were proof that Vittore had taken an active part in Lio's care. She walked on, down the room, absorbing this fact. At the same time she was trying to deal with the fact that some of the pictures had made her heart sink.

Amid the shots of Vittore and Lio had been many with assorted groups of people. Probably part of the extended family. But it was the ones of her nephew with beautiful women which had dampened her spirits.

She hadn't seen them properly, but one woman had definitely been a stunning blonde. Another was dark with a figure to die for. Verity frowned, hoping they were relatives. But she wasn't holding her breath.

She knew what Vittore was like. He adored women and they adored him. That would never change. If Lio settled down in Italy, Vittore would almost certainly have several affairs during his son's childhood.

She went cold and her hand tightened around Lio's in alarm as she thought of the consequences. He'd just get used to one of his father's mistresses when another one would appear on the scene. Where was the stability in that? All his life, women would be abandoning him. It made her shiver to think of the kind of man he'd become.

She looked down on his sweet blond head, agonising that one day he'd be cold and hard and contemptuous. All innocence, he smiled up at her trustingly.

'Sossoss?' he asked hopefully.

'Sausages?' she said with a smile, a break in her voice. 'Shall we see?'

Lio nodded. Dear heaven, she thought shakily. He meant the world to her. She was his rock. It had been left to her to protect him and if that meant defying Vittore and his rights and his wealth and his wretched harem then that's what she'd do!

Braced for battle, she came out into the sunshine and stood for a moment, blinking. At the far end of the terrace, Vittore rose, his eyes misty for a moment as they fixed on Lio. And then he turned his glance to Verity.

'I could leave if you think it necessary,' he said, very quietly.

She looked down at her nephew.

'Sossoss?' he asked, jiggling up and down.

She laughed. 'You and your tummy!' Confident in Lio's love, she said magnanimously, 'I think L-I-O is doing all right at the moment. Hunger has overcome his fear of you. He's keen to eat his breakfast,' she added with a laugh. 'Oops! Prove me wrong, then! Where are you going, sweetheart?' she cried, as Lio suddenly tore his hand from hers.

''Ook!' Excitedly he pointed at the fountain, burbling below the flight of steps into the garden.

'Look,' she encouraged. 'Water. You like water, Lio.'

To Verity's delight, he started on a laborious and careful climb down the steps without demanding that she followed. She watched lovingly as he reached up and paddled his hands in the fountain, quite astonished that he should have left her side in such a strange place.

And then the implications hit home. Her heart began to race. Lio was settling in too quickly, too well! She gulped, afraid of what that meant.

It was good. It was right, she told herself. And if his excessive anxiety vanished then she would be pleased. Her mouth wobbled and she jammed her teeth together hard.

Her interests, her needs weren't important. She must be glad for Lio if his emotional problems were resolved.

Except that it meant he might be happy to be with Vittore. And would therefore be prey to Vittore's stream of women.

She would be asked to leave. Perhaps she'd be going home before the six months were up. And in that case… Her eyes became huge with alarm. Vittore would claim his bet. He'd have the right to make love to her. Until the novelty wore off.

She went pale with horror. How had she ever agreed to such a medieval arrangement?

CHAPTER SEVEN

SHE glanced warily at Vittore, chills running up and down her spine. He was opening a huge canopy over the breakfast table to provide shade for them, his delighted smile illuminating his face. And despite herself, she felt the warmth of his happiness enclose her heart.

His inky eyes met hers. 'He's not daunted,' he said softly, though his curbed exuberance was unmistakable. 'He likes it here!'

Verity moved towards him, her mind a mass of contradictions.

'It seems you may have made the right decision after all,' she agreed stiffly.

'Be glad for him.'

She sighed. 'I am.'

Their gazes held. They both knew what this could mean. Vittore would gain everything. She would lose all that she valued dearly.

'Oh! *Tesoruccio mio!*' whispered a voice from within the salon.

The spell between them was broken. Verity turned her head to see a plump, dark-haired woman dressed entirely in black emerging with a laden trolley. Her tearful eyes were fixed on Lio and a stream of softly passionate Italian poured from her mouth.

'Hush, Maria!' Vittore's arm came around the woman and he proffered his handkerchief. '*Calma, calma!*' he soothed quietly, giving the broad black shoulders a squeeze. 'Verity,' he said quietly. 'This is Maria, my housekeeper. Maria, this is Verity, Linda's sister, who looked after Lio—'

Before she could say anything, Verity found herself wrapped in a bear hug, her ears assailed by one whispered '*grazie!*' after another.

'You bring our baby back,' Maria said in a whisper, drawing back and letting Verity breathe again. 'We are so happy! You make *il conte* smile again. I kiss you. I thank you. And now,' sniffed Maria, 'I bring you the big breakfast. The baby, he is so sweet. So lovely...and yes, yes, I know,' she breathed, eyeing the oblivious Lio fondly. 'I will not go to him. I wait. I go now. But I kiss you again...'

'Thank you, Maria,' Verity said with a warm smile, overwhelmed by the woman's joy. 'You're very kind.'

'Ah. You are beautiful. In here.' Maria banged her capacious bosom dramatically. 'Not like your sister. Hah!'

'Maria!' Vittore's tone was low and kindly, but held a warning.

'Yes, I go, I go! I am happy. You are happy. We all are happy!'

Maria moved with a dancer's grace to Vittore who had sat down at the table, clapped a huge and comforting hand on his shoulder and vanished back into the salon.

'Your staff are very fond of you,' Verity commented slowly, watching Lio solemnly flicking water at the cherub in the middle of the fountain.

'And I of them. They've known me all my life.' He seemed to be gauging her reaction to that piece of information.

'Oh.' Her face grew thoughtful.

You couldn't buy that kind of loyalty or affection. Unless, of course, Vittore had kept his flagrant infidelity a secret. She frowned, struggling with the conflicting information.

'Would Maria be fond of me,' Vittore said quietly, 'if I had neglected Lio?'

She blinked, startled by the question and thought of those happy, fatherly photographs. A man besotted with his child.

'No,' she answered honestly.

'So Linda lied about me.'

She chewed her lip. 'It looks like it,' she said slowly.

'And if she told that lie…?'

Verity felt her pulses quicken. Yes. If Linda had lied about the relationship between Vittore and Lio, had she also lied about the women who had warmed his bed? Or was she kidding herself? Was that what she wanted to be true?

'Lio's coming back,' Vittore said quietly, breaking in on her frenzied thoughts.

'Thanks,' she whispered, moving to the top of the steps.

As she waited for Lio, she was astonished at how badly she wanted Vittore to have been faithful and true. But it was unlikely. Men with devastating good looks always had plenty of opportunities to stray. And Vittore had wealth and charm by the bucket-load.

She felt less sure of herself now. And less certain that Lio would reject Vittore. Remembering the pact she'd agreed to, she shivered, hating the thought of being used for sex. And even more terrified that she and Lio would be parted.

Her mind in turmoil, she responded to Lio's insistent 'Up!' and lifted him into her arms. To divert him, she investigated the silver lidded dishes on the trolley, marvelling at the wonderful breakfast that Maria had prepared.

'Sossoss!' protested Lio excitedly, wriggling.

'You and your sausages!' teased Verity. 'All right, squiggly worm. Sit in the chair and—'

Lio began to grizzle and indicate that he wanted to sit on Verity's lap.

'No, *caro*,' Vittore said very softly. 'This is where you eat. Maria brought it especially, from her daughter's house.'

With firm but gentle hands, he managed to fold the surprised Lio's legs beneath the tray of the high chair and had snapped on the harness before his son could protest. In fact, when Lio opened his mouth to yell, Vittore boldly popped a sausage in there.

Verity watched the battle going on in Lio's mind as his small teeth clamped around the sausage. Should he register his protest, or enjoy his favourite food? Another sausage appeared enticingly on a teddy bear plate in front of Lio and then Vittore walked off whistling casually, disappearing through the salon door.

It was too much for a hungry child to bear. With the object of his anger gone, Lio settled down to his breakfast. And, after adding bacon and egg to his plate, Verity indulged herself too, pointing out birds and butterflies to the contentedly munching Lio and fearfully afraid that perhaps—just perhaps—she'd been handling him badly all along.

Vittore had made it look so easy. Though, she argued, *she'd* never been able to walk away from Lio like that. There would have been tears. She speared a herby sausage reflectively. Let Vittore try to cope with Lio on his own—then he'd find out what problems there were.

After breakfast, she and Lio remained in the garden, staying on the upper level which had been child-proofed by a gate which cut it off from the other terraces. They played in the sandpit and she kept glancing up to dream over the incomparable view of the glittering blue sea.

Perhaps an hour later, a small inflated paddling pool was cautiously pushed around the corner of a hedge. Verity giggled when the end of a hose snaked into the pool and began to fill it.

Lio was so engrossed in filling a sieve with sand that he only noticed what was going on when a duck, a bucket and a boat collided together in mid-air as they arced towards the water.

Squawking with delight, he ran towards the pool eagerly. A laughing Verity just managed to reach him in time to stop him from flinging himself in fully clothed. There was a chuckle from behind the hedge which she recognised as Vittore's. And a large towel landed close by her feet.

'Thanks,' she whispered, amused by the subterfuge, but there was no reply.

By noon, Lio was exhausted from splashing everything in sight. Although he rubbed his eyes furiously he stubbornly refused to curl up with her for his morning nap.

Frustrated with the yelling child, Verity saw that her friendly hedge had sprouted a hand. And in that hand waved two of Lio's favourite books.

Once recovered, the books were read and their buttons pushed to produce the music Lio loved. And slowly his eyes closed and his head rolled. He was asleep.

Verity peered at the hedge hopefully. She smiled when Vittore appeared with a rug, which he placed in the shade of a huge olive tree.

'You saved me,' she said gratefully.

'He needs two people to look after him,' Vittore observed.

'So I realise,' she replied, sobered.

'Let me have him. I want to hold him for a moment. Then I'll put him down to sleep on the rug.'

It would be churlish to refuse. 'OK.' She held out her nephew who grumbled in his light sleep and flailed his arms around.

'Vittore!' purred someone on the terrace behind them.

She turned. Saw someone young and slender with long, straight brown legs and equally long brown hair that gleamed healthily in the sunlight. Someone who looked desperately elegant in an understated, simple shift—

'Bianca!' cried Vittore softly, his whole tone and body and expression bathed in love and delight.

Verity felt the muscles of her chest jack-knife. This was one of the women who'd been photographed with baby Lio. This was Bianca, then.

And to her astonishment, Vittore abandoned his supposedly adored son and strode jauntily towards the terrace.

Her head snapped back again, sitting tensely on her stiff neck. So, she thought waspishly, deliberately not looking around. The mistress that Linda had mentioned. She'd been around when Lio was tiny. And still had a hold on Vittore, it seemed.

She imagined their kisses, the way he was holding Bianca in his arms and gazing down at his mistress, murmuring satin compliments. So much for Vittore's priorities. Women first, Lio second. It was as she'd thought.

Grim-faced, she gently laid Lio down and stalked off a few yards to stare at the view, arranging herself as elegantly as she could out of sheer pride.

But she couldn't see much for the red mist in front of her eyes. And she was scared, too, scared to meet the woman who had ruined Linda's marriage and had made Lio a bewildered little boy instead of a happy and contented child.

Tensely she waited, her body as rigid as a steel girder. Her ears strained to catch the sounds she expected: Vittore and Bianca talking, walking arm in arm across the lawn, pausing to admire his son and then—because Bianca was a woman, wasn't she, and would be curious about Lio's aunt—they would come over to chat.

Well, it would be one-sided. She could hardly speak for angry tears. Vittore's protestations of devotion to Lio had been flung to the four winds by a woman's siren call.

Loathsome man! Impulsively she whirled, intending to confront him with this, fire blazing in her hot eyes.

He and Bianca had disappeared.

Rage swelled her chest. They'd probably gone to bed. That's what mistresses were for, after all!

Thinking of him, naked, arms and legs tangling with Bianca's, his mouth roaming everywhere in passionate and arousing kisses, she wanted to stamp her feet with the frustration that rampaged through her.

Yet she could do nothing, go nowhere, couldn't even run to the hall and yell something rude, witty or pithy in the direction of the bedrooms above. Not that she'd stoop so low—however much she wanted to.

Lio held her here. She had to stay with him.

'That settles it. It's you and me, sweetheart,' she muttered crossly, sinking to the rug beside him. 'Your father was just a sperm bank as far as you're concerned. He won't put you first, above everything and everyone else. Poor Linda,' she mused. 'I know how she felt, now and why she couldn't trust Vittore to care for you properly. And as for Bianca turning up and whisking Vittore off to bed...! Talk about blatant!' she whispered fiercely. 'You know, I haven't even *slept* with your father, but I feel humiliated seeing him disappear with another woman, after he tried to seduce me. I suppose I was just a stop-gap. No wonder your mother escaped. Vittore is an insensitive *louse!*'

Her mouth compressed. She lay down and stared at the sky, trying not to imagine what Bianca was doing and how well she was doing it. She cared, she thought miserably. She really minded that Vittore was a rat and a selfish, twenty-timing rotter.

Some hours later, in the dimly lit nursery, she knew Vittore and Bianca were by the door but she stayed rigidly beside Lio's cot which had miraculously appeared, checking that he was fully asleep. Her skin prickled with tension and every muscle in her body quivered with strain.

Was Bianca looking triumphantly sultry in the aftermath of sex? Did Vittore have his arm around the woman protectively and was he smug? She wanted to clench her fists and grind her teeth and stamp her feet. But she stood there, ostensibly stroking Lio's small body and trying to master the green-eyed monster who'd taken up residence in her brain.

'Che bello!' sighed a soft voice.

Definitely Bianca. Verity made a point of checking her watch. Eight o'clock. She wondered what time supper was served and if she'd be forced to sit at the same table as

Vittore's mistress. If so, she wouldn't be able to eat a thing. Her stomach already felt as if builders were digging foundations in there. It was a novel way to diet.

'Verity, this is Bianca,' Vittore said lovingly.

She experienced a sour and bitter sensation in her gut. 'I know.'

Unable to face the woman, she kept her back to Vittore's paramour and did busy things, straightening the sheet, tugging at the pillow, adjusting the bumper cushions.

'Hello, Verity,' the unnaturally sweet Bianca cooed.

'Shh!' Verity scolded with a frown. And felt ashamed of acting like a petulant child, even though she couldn't stop herself.

'Is he asleep now?' Vittore touched her arm, unexpectedly just behind her shoulder.

She shrugged his hand away. 'Just about,' she muttered grudgingly.

He bent low, and to Verity's jaundiced eyes it seemed that he assumed a look of utter devotion with suspiciously slick ease.

'Come and see, Bianca,' he murmured. 'He's so beautiful.'

'Oh, yes!' Bianca whispered ecstatically.

Verity froze, the hairs standing up on her neck. Not in a million years!

'Stay there!' she hissed.

'I thought he was asl—'

Verity flashed an irritated glance over her shoulder that cut off Bianca's protest abruptly. She saw that the woman was in her twenties, with a flawless olive complexion and such dark eyes and white teeth that she didn't need any make up at all. Verity loathed her on sight.

'He can be restless at first and sometimes wakes. I don't want him disturbed.' She scowled. 'If he opens his eyes and sees you, he'll panic.'

Vittore nodded at the disappointed Bianca. 'You'll see

enough of him as time goes on,' he said with great tenderness.

Not if she could help it, Verity thought darkly. 'I would like you *both* to leave,' she said bossily.

'Not yet. I've hardly had a moment—' Vittore began.

'You could have stayed with him when he fell asleep this morning,' Verity snapped before she could stop herself.

He slanted a glance at Bianca, a flush on his cheeks. Guilt, Verity thought, her stomach churning horribly like a cement mixer.

Bianca produced an angelic smile. 'My fault, I am afraid,' she said in an attractively husky voice.

Verity met her innocent gaze with hard eyes. 'That's what I thought.'

'You see—' Bianca began.

'Please don't explain,' Verity said hastily.

'Cara,' Vittore murmured, taking the woman's arm and leading her to the door.

He spoke in Italian to her and when she kissed him on both cheeks and left, he turned back to Verity who was intently folding Lio's grubby clothes into maniacally neat shapes and then tossing them anyhow into the laundry basket by the bathroom door before realising that Vittore was finding this pointless activity very amusing.

Suddenly seeing her reflection in the bathroom mirror, she discovered to her horror that the exertions of the day had taken their toll on her.

There was nothing smooth or elegant about her tumbling, tangled curls, or the grass and dead flowers which adorned them—courtesy of Lio. Her dress was stained from the peaches that Lio had dropped down her bodice during lunch and there was something horribly like toothpaste glistening at the corner of her mouth. Thanks to showing one little boy how to brush his teeth properly.

She let out a small groan and whisked the offending toothpaste away with her finger.

'You're upset,' Vittore observed.

She flung up her head in denial, sending her hair and half the countryside flying in all directions.

'Am I?' she grumbled.

He smiled knowingly, annoying her still further. 'You know you are. Because of Bianca.'

'Who? Oh. Her. Why should she bother me?'

He took Lio's toy car from her and she blushed because she'd been grimly grinding it backwards and forwards over the palm of her hand.

'That's what I find so fascinating,' he said quietly.

Too close, her defences warned her. Already her skin burned, her hands were poised to capture his face and bring it to hers for a kiss that would drive the wretched Bianca from his mind once and for all.

Verity groaned again and hastily turned away but Vittore was too quick for her. His hands pulled her around again, his eyes intense and dark, drawing her inexorably in to his force field, commanding her, making a hash of her brain.

'Listen to me,' he said quietly.

She stared at his chest, listening instead to the voices inside her which tempted her to abandon herself to him and be done with it.

'And hear more lies?' she creaked out.

He sighed. 'I want you to believe me but I don't know how to convince you. All I can say is that Bianca is not my mistress. And never has been.'

She managed to shrug even though his warm breath was whispering tantalisingly on her face and she longed to ease her starved mouth with his.

For a moment, her lips were so dry that she struggled to answer. Surreptitiously she let her tongue slither out to moisten them. And she felt Vittore stiffen, his breathing more hectic than ever.

She responded. Oh, how she responded. Every inch, every minute particle of her lived for him. The caress of his fingers on her arms maddened her. And why did he have to look at her like that? Ice would melt beneath that dark, sultry gaze, so redolent of sexual promise.

But she wouldn't succumb. Somehow she met his feral gaze with scorn which she'd dredged up from goodness knew where.

'As I said. Why should I care either way what Bianca is to you?'

'I don't know. You tell me,' he murmured.

'It's not personal, just a moral thing. She broke up your marriage. I don't like the idea of Lio being exposed to someone like her.'

'She didn't break up my marriage,' he said quietly. 'And I don't want to talk about that. I want you to be fair to Bianca—not to prejudge her.'

'I made my wishes clear,' she retorted. 'I don't want strangers hanging around Lio.'

'But he was asleep.'

'Only just. And therefore easily woken,' she argued.

'Yes. Which is why I hurried over to Bianca when she first arrived this afternoon, to stop her calling out again,' he said, his eyes intent on her. When she looked at him in disbelief, he said gently, 'I took the opportunity to explain about Lio and then we discussed urgent business. I have changes to make in my life. You know that. And the sooner the better.'

Verity wondered why she was twisting Lio's little socks into corkscrews. Perhaps, she thought morosely, it stopped her from running her hands over Vittore's heaving chest to see if his heart beat as frenetically as hers.

'Did you tell her about our arrangement?' she enquired coldly.

'The six-month deadline? I think that's between us, don't you?' he murmured, brushing her cheek with the back of his hand.

She shuddered and her eyes half-closed as his head angled, the arch of his mouth too sensual to resist. Exquisite tremors whirred along her nerves, peaking her breasts and feeding her contracting womb with moist excitement.

'Vittore,' someone whispered huskily.

'I'll show you your room,' he said, suddenly quite cool and detached. 'It's next to the nursery and has a portable video link so you can check on Lio. You can change for dinner and come straight down. This way.'

Dazed and battered and incredibly aroused, she felt him tugging her along like a sullen child denied sweets. She was in his power, she thought hopelessly. Snared, hook line and sinker.

Tingling from an ice cold shower and wishing she'd packed a chastity belt, she stomped reluctantly down the stairs towards the sound of laughter. One male, one female. Vittore and, presumably, the luscious Bianca.

Vanity prompted her to draw herself up to slim her waist as much as possible and she checked that her hair was still vaguely where she'd hurriedly pinned it up on top of her head. It had been brushed with a ferocity more suited to a concrete floor, and her scalp positively glowed.

The long tangerine skirt that floated about her legs was hardly a match for the lovely Bianca's understated elegance, nor for that matter was the low-cut scarlet top. But she'd chosen the items deliberately, to be bright and bold. To make a statement.

'Signorina Ferty! La sala da pranzo! To eat! Is here!' An excited Maria was indicating a door to the left of the hall.

Verity smiled. 'Thank you, Maria. *Grazie,*' she said as an afterthought, exhausting virtually all the Italian she knew.

'Prego.' Maria rubbed her hands happily on her apron and hurried off.

This was it. Verity drew a deep breath then strode in, her eyes afire with challenge, legs fluid beneath the soft and vibrant skirt.

She saw the room first. Vast, panelled, beautifully furnished and dominated by a long, gleaming mahogany table lit by silver candelabra. The facets of wine glasses sparkled, gold-rimmed plates and heavy silver cutlery gleamed in the flickering golden light.

And then she saw Vittore, who'd noticed her hovering in the doorway and had risen, his eyes dark with a stupefying desire—though that was most probably for the blonde sitting opposite him with her back to the door.

The blonde in the photo, she thought in agitation, recognising the style and colour of the woman's hair at once. How many of these women did he keep going at a time? He was like a juggler in a travelling circus—

'Wow!' cried the woman, her head now turned in Verity's direction.

Verity blinked in confusion, seeing his companion clearly for the first time. The corners of her mouth twitched and she placed the baby alarm on a side table, her pansy eyes dancing.

'Snap!' she said with a laugh, eyeing the woman's outfit.

The stranger, of uncertain age, had arranged her blond hair into a very trendy top-knot that stuck out at all angles. She grinned, leapt from her chair and came forward, dazzling in her long cinnamon skirt and poppy-red top which was almost identical to Verity's.

'Verity,' she said warmly, holding out her hands.

And without knowing why, Verity found herself walking into the woman's embrace and gasping from the bear hug which followed.

'How wonderful!' sighed the blonde, pushing Verity back a little and examining her in detail. 'A kindred spirit at last!'

Verity did the same, establishing what she'd instinctively known already; that this was not another of Vittore's women because there were deep laughter lines around the blue eyes and mobile mouth which had taken some time to get there.

'Mother—' began Vittore.

'Oh! Yes!' The woman laughed and the lines danced attractively. 'I'm Honesty, Vittore's mother. Stupid name, isn't it? But I'm stuck with it. Maria calls me *La contessa Onsty*, which taxes her teeth somewhat. And you're Verity and so, so welcome! He never said you were beautiful, but then he was bowled over by the excitement of bringing Lio home. I can understand that. I watched the two of you from the window earlier, playing in the garden. He's adorable. I can't wait to get my hands on him! And you were so good with him. I can see you care for my grandson deeply. I'm so glad you're going to be here for a few months while he settles in.'

Verity opened her mouth to make the situation clear, anxious that Vittore's mother didn't get the wrong idea, but already she was rushing on in her excitable, unstoppable way.

'...and you're interested in plants, too, aren't you? I couldn't help but notice that you examined them with great interest and—'

'Mother,' interrupted Vittore politely.

Honesty laughed and grinned at him fondly. 'He's so commanding. Just like his father. Now,' she said, guiding the amused Verity to the table, 'let's eat. I'm starving. We'll have to take turns talking, so we actually get a calorie or two down us. Why,' she demanded, hardly drawing breath as she waved Verity to a chair and sat down herself, robustly attacking a bread stick, 'are you interested in gardens? Vittore was conceived in this one, beneath the mimosa. I've had a fondness for it and shooting stars ever since. Do you have a garden yourself? What's it like? Do you favour Gertrude Jekyll or—?'

'Mother,' murmured Vittore, his hand affectionately covering Honesty's, 'perhaps you could allow Verity to answer *one* of those questions?'

'He thinks Italians are the only passionate people in the world,' Honesty confided, leaning towards Verity. 'But we know different, don't we? Your turn,' she finished abruptly, and beamed expectantly.

Verity's eyes glowed. Yes. She liked this woman. 'I have questions of my own, first.'

'Fire them at me. Oh! Maria! Spaghetti and clams! My favourite, along with risotto. We eat that *all'onda* here—like the wave, so that it ripples when you shake the pan. It's a very Naples thing. I'll teach you how to make that sometime. But now, try this, Verity. The tomato sauce is to die for. You'll have to talk at the same time.'

'If she's allowed,' drawled Vittore.

Suppressing a giggle, Verity waited till Maria had placed a heaped plate in front of her and then asked, 'You're English, er…Honesty?'

'As they come. Met Arturo—Vittore's father—when I interviewed him for the magazine I worked for. I'd intended to write a scathing article about the shallow, irrelevant world of fashion and ended up praising his humanity and astuteness to the skies and losing my ability to walk.'

'Oh!' Verity looked shocked. 'How awful!'

'I think she means,' interjected Vittore softly, 'that her knees went weak at the sight of Father.' He smiled at Verity and raised a meaningful eyebrow when she blushed, half-afraid that he knew the perilous state of her own knees.

'And I never recovered,' sighed Honesty, not noticing any of the by-play. 'Odd how love can hit you like a sledgehammer. They say there's no such thing as love at first sight, but boy, can I prove them wrong! It's no use fighting it. I tried, because I was hell-bent on becoming journalist of the year one day, but I kept weeping into my tea and diluting it till it tasted vile so I gave in to the inevitable.'

Flustered, Verity flicked a quick glance at Vittore. He was looking at her thoughtfully and his eyes kindled when their gazes met.

'Ask her about Bianca,' he said huskily.

'Oh, such a sweet girl!' Honesty enthused, needing no asking. 'You'll like her. Straightforward, loyal, hard working and totally without guile. Of course, she'd been earmarked for Vittore years ago when she was still in her pram. Two dynasties would have been joined with their marriage. They were about to become engaged when Arturo died. Two months later, Vittore had married your sister instead. I've no idea why,' she said candidly. 'They had nothing in common. You haven't told me about your gardening interest,' she accused, frowning at Verity.

'Why don't you concentrate on eating, Mother and let Verity speak?' Vittore was frowning. Evidently he wasn't too pleased with his mother's revelation.

'Bianca spends a lot of time here, does she?' Verity asked as Honesty was opening her mouth to reply.

'Second home when she's not working. She and Vittore are like *that*.' Honesty twisted her middle finger over her forefinger. 'Nothing sexual of course. Brother and sister. No spark, you see. She and Vittore meet often because she's doing his job so he can concentrate on the children.'

Verity's head was reeling. 'Children?' she asked faintly, imagining dozens of illegitimate babies spread all over Italy.

'Well, there's an awful lot of them now,' Honesty said quite shamelessly. 'It all began when Lio disappeared and Tore roared around like a wounded bull for weeks on end. Maria and I stopped weeping on one another's shoulders and started worrying about Vittore. We shouted at him and bullied him until he came down to earth again. And I suggested that he should hurl all his pain and energy into helping children with special needs. Anyway, he's set up these centres—no, Maria! I haven't finished! Do come back in a moment! I know, but it's delicious. You're a treasure. Where was I? Centres…yes, all over the world, which cater for severely handicapped children and give them education, physiotherapy, a home, hope, holidays, oh, a *life*. You should see their progress, their happiness! It's heart-warming… Yes, Vittore. I'm eating, look! You tell me things, Verity. About yourself. I can't hog the conversation all the time.'

'Are you sure? You've succeeded so far,' Vittore drawled. His mother grinned, quite unperturbed.

Verity was staring at him, bewildered by what she'd heard. It seemed inconceivable that Vittore could do something so worthy, so touchingly *good*. Nothing was making sense any longer. Perhaps he wasn't the shallow, clothes-mad, spoilt Lothario she'd imagined.

Though, she mused cynically, he could still be nice to children and yet try to bed every reasonable-looking woman he met.

And something else had caught her attention. Vittore's mother had claimed that no spark existed between him and Bianca. Could that be true? She tried to think of their behaviour objectively. There was certainly love of a kind. Surely Bianca must adore him? And he'd take advantage of that, any man would.

She saw Honesty was waiting for her to speak and, realising this was unusual, she found herself forgetting Bianca and smiling back at the friendly, enthusiastic woman.

'You want to hear about my background. There isn't much. I suppose you know I was adopted. I went off to study at a horticultural college and lost touch with Linda. I'm a landscape gardener. I love the garden here. It's everything I adore.' Honesty beamed at her and Verity continued, quite relaxed and comfortable despite the grand surroundings. 'Before I stopped work to look after Lio,' she confided, 'I'd built up a good clientele in London and had become fashionably in demand, though I found that most of my work was a little repetitive because some things were "in" and some were "out" and I like more freedom than that.'

'My style, too. I can tell from the way you're dressed,' said Honesty, allowing Maria to remove her plate at last. 'You're not inhibited or repressed, are you? Not with that hair tumbling about. No, don't stuff it up! Let it cascade. I envy you the colour. Mine's tinted. Pure white underneath but I'm not ready to look old yet,' she said with a devastating frankness. 'Yours is beautiful. Isn't it, Vittore?'

'Yes.'

His mother frowned. 'What's the matter with you? Fling compliments at her! She's gorgeous! Where are your manners?'

'I'm saving Verity's blushes,' he said drily.

'Well, she's gone bright red, so you haven't succeeded,' Honesty retorted tartly. *'Ohhh!'* she squealed, leaping to her feet in horror.

'What is it?' cried Vittore in alarm.

'My cuttings!' She flung down her napkin in haste and pushed back her chair. 'I forgot to spray them!'

'Good grief! Plant cuttings! I thought you'd been bitten by a nest of vipers at the very least.' He subsided into his seat again with an indulgent grin. 'Can't someone else—?'

Vittore's suggestion was waved away with an impatient hand. 'I wouldn't trust anyone with them,' his mother said firmly. 'Got to go. See you again. You understand, Verity, don't you? Plants, like children and love, need nurturing. *Ciao*, darling.' She blew kisses. 'Bye, Verity. Can't wait to talk gardens with you. I'm in awe of your talent. We'll plan something new for the garden, shall we? Surprise Vittore. Must dash. *Love* your dress sense!'

'Drive carefully, Mother!' admonished Vittore, rising again and accompanying her to the door.

'You bet. I wouldn't want to die now, darling,' she assured him, 'not with my grandson to enjoy. Shoo. Get on with your meal. You have a guest. I can let myself out. Byeee!'

Vittore turned, his face wreathed in fond smiles. 'Dear Mother. Do you feel as if you've been flattened by a steamroller?' he asked Verity, returning to his seat.

She laughed. 'She's a one-woman hurricane! But she's

wonderful, Vittore. Not at all the kind of person I was expecting.'

'I hoped you'd like her. Maybe you've got me wrong, too,' he said quietly.

She was silent while a dish of lamb was brought in. Maybe she had. But how would she ever know?

An hour later, after the lamb, some rich, crumbly cheese and choux pastry filled with a kind of custard and topped with wild cherries, she had ditched her caution and—perhaps influenced by the appropriately named Honesty—was just being herself.

It was a wonderful relief. She could let rip and say what she thought, flinging phrases at Vittore that made him roar with laughter. Suddenly she felt witty and more alive than at any time in her life. She loved making him laugh. He did it with utter abandon and came back at her with amusing remarks and tales that meant they were both weak with laughter by the time tiny cups of espresso arrived.

'Thanks, Maria,' he said fondly, his face bright with pleasure. 'Fantastic meal, as usual.' He kissed his fingers in appreciation. To Verity's surprise, Maria dropped a heavy kiss on Vittore's forehead. He smiled up at the housekeeper as if this were nothing unusual. 'Leave all this,' he said. 'It can wait till the morning. *'Sera.'*

'Buona sera. Buona sera, signorina Ferty.'

Verity beamed. She felt as if she was glowing.

'Goodnight, Maria. Thank you for the lovely meal. You are a marvellous cook.'

'No, no!' Maria dismissed. 'I cook with love. For good man.'

'Yes. I understand,' Verity said quietly.

It was obvious that every dish had been made with loving care by Maria for the employer she adored unconditionally. That was significant.

Verity watched the housekeeper leave, every inch of her bustling with pride, and felt a new warmth towards Vittore.

So far, there had been no evidence to support Linda's accusations.

And yet Linda had fled. Sipping her wine thoughtfully, Verity decided to see if Honesty could shed light on that. At least, she thought in amusement, Vittore's mother would be frank and wouldn't clam up!

Vittore pushed back his chair and stood up. He pocketed the baby monitor then picked up the tray of coffee and chocolate truffles.

'Shall we have these outside?' he suggested. 'The angels' trumpets smell wonderful at night.'

'Brugmansia? I love them. Where are they?' she cried eagerly, thinking ruefully as she asked that he knew just how to tempt her into the magical night.

But she followed, nevertheless, heartened by the wonderful food and the warm, family atmosphere. She had to admit that she'd been wrong about the move to Italy. This would be the perfect place for Lio to grow up—provided Linda had lied about Vittore being addicted to sex.

'Come.'

Vittore held out his free hand. She had meant to refuse it, but found herself moving forwards and slipping her hot hand in his. In silence they walked across the lawn. Moonlight sifted through the trees and the huge bowl of the starry sky seemed as dense as black velvet.

Vittore's grip tightened. She felt right, strolling beside him, as though they'd been together for a lifetime. It was the romantic night that seduced her, of course, she told herself. Plus the pleasure of talking with someone on her wavelength. The fun they'd had over dinner. Two glasses of wine.

She stumbled and his arm slid around her waist to steady her. There it stayed and she made no effort to move away from his embrace because she was standing enraptured by the view.

They stood high above the sea, the gentle waves whispering on the sandy shore of a small cove. The Amalfi Bay stretched in a loving curve, its shape only discernible by the twinkling lights around its edges and on the almost vertical hills above.

The exotic sound of thousands of cicadas whirred in her head and the sharp lemon scent of white angels' trumpets almost overpowered her senses.

Vittore put the tray on a small wrought iron table and handed her the tiny cup of espresso. She bent her head and sipped, thinking that this dark, rich—almost chocolate—flavour was just one more sensual attack on her vulnerable body.

She seemed to be closer to him. Had she moved or had he? She couldn't speak, couldn't move now, that was for sure. The empty cup was removed from her shaking hand. A truffle offered to her mouth.

Blind with the beauty of it all, she obediently parted her lips and let Vittore slip the chocolate in. His fingers lingered. Traced a nerve-tingling path to the corner of her mouth as the explosions of taste melted deliciously on her tongue.

There was the lightest of kisses on her lips. The faintest sensation of electrifying excitement when the tip of his tongue brushed along her mouth. And then he had drawn back, his eyes hungry in the darkness.

'Time you were in bed,' he said huskily.

She swallowed and tried to find indignation at the loaded suggestion. But all she could manage was a throaty croak.

'I know,' he murmured. 'I could stay out here all night too. But you need your sleep. Lio is hard work. I'll walk you back.'

Verity was so astonished that she didn't resist when he politely took her elbow and strolled back through the garden with her. This was good, she tried to tell herself. But contrarily, she felt disappointed that he wasn't even going to make a pass. He'd set up that madly erotic moment, when her senses were totally overwhelmed, and he hadn't capitalised on it.

She burned. Everywhere. Felt unfinished, a desperate ache filling the sweet, moist core of her body which angrily urged her to slither seductively against him and torment him beyond all control.

He shouldn't be so indifferent. It wasn't right! How dared he turn her on and not follow through? And now they'd reached the house. Soon he'd leave her and she'd be left in her room, frantic with need.

'Goodnight,' he breathed.

She should be glad. Tried hard to feel relief. Instead, she bristled, mortally offended. Her eyes lifted to his in unconscious reproach. Hot violet melted under his dark gaze.

'Night,' she said in a pathetic husk.

It seemed he couldn't go. She didn't know how long they stood there, bound by the incredible heat that they generated together. Only that she became more and more liquid as the temperature rose, her breathing more erratic, her desire total.

Suddenly in her desperation she reached up and drew down his head, a groan escaping from her as their mouths met in an explosive kiss that rocked her on her feet.

His passion erupted. She was on the ground beneath him, the weight of his body and his grinding mouth everything that she had wanted to relieve the terrible wanting. Their arms and legs sought to trap one another in frantic movements and soon she hardly knew where her body ended and his began.

His mouth was on her breast. Hot, urgent, infinitely sweet. She arched her back and moaned, pressing herself against him, eager it seemed to become part of his body.

She felt her dress being peeled down to her waist so that his avid lips could explore her bare, tingling skin. Then his hands began to caress her legs, moving far too slowly upwards while she writhed and encouraged him with biting kisses, moans and little begging pleas.

She adored his mouth. Adored his body, its clean, male smell, the silk of his hair, the feel of the muscles beneath the skin. Her fingers, mouth and teeth learnt him as her womanhood clamoured for more and more.

She heard a groan rip from his throat and then there were no more fingers creating unbelievable delights, no hard thighs gripping her tightly, no swooping mouth satisfying her with such sweet roughness.

Her eyes opened. His lashes were lowered and he was awkwardly settling her bodice back into its proper place, the line of his jaw hard as if his teeth were clenched like a vice.

Humiliation washed over her. Not only had she lost her head and invited his kisses, but he'd discovered that he wasn't interested in her after all! And this was a man who adored women and everything that they had to offer!

Perhaps he *did* only want to snare her to gain Lio's confidence, and he hadn't bargained on her taking the situation so far.

Groggily she sat up. Ignored his silently offered hand and scrambled clumsily to her feet.

'Verity—'

Her flapping hand stopped him. Told him not to speak. She could talk with her hands, too, she thought miserably.

And she wove her unsteady way to the hall and the safety of her virgin bed, every part of her throbbing and reminding her that if she'd been more alluring she could have been lying in Vittore's arms listening to the cicadas' siren songs and the soft wash of the waves with the night sky above and its sequin stars.

She tried to tell herself that she'd had a lucky escape. That he'd only ever made passes at her to keep her sweet and to encourage Lio to see him as a friend. But common sense and rational thinking made little headway in her brain. She still wished she was Vittore's prisoner, trapped beneath his warm, powerful body, moving to the eternal rhythm of man and woman.

How stupid, she thought forlornly, dragging off her clothes and slipping naked between the cool, caressing sheets. She'd fallen for the silken charm of a rake with an agenda on his mind, and she had become wanton in her desperation.

But it wasn't love that she felt, only sexual desire. And in the morning she'd be thankful that she was still intact.

She frowned. Her breasts ached. Touching them, she closed her eyes and remembered Vittore's teeth there, gently tugging. Horrified, she hurriedly flung her arms by her sides and lay as stiff as starch, willing the wonderful, wicked sensations to leave her starving body.

CHAPTER EIGHT

IT WAS a long time before the cascade of freezing water had eased his physical craving and he could step out of the shower. Cold showers had become an essential part of his life, he thought wryly.

Unfortunately nothing seemed to diminish his hectic thoughts. Over and over again for hour after hour he paced up and down, replaying the scenes of that day he'd spent with Verity, reliving the pleasure he had taken in touching, tasting, and looking at her inflammatory body.

No matter what he did, she wouldn't get out of his head. Her laughing face, and gurgles of delight over dinner as they'd bandied words about, just stayed fixed in his mind, tormenting him relentlessly until he felt he must be going mad.

Angrily he sprawled on the bed, staring at the ceiling and wishing the night away. After Linda, he had vowed that no woman would ever get to him again. But this one was really touching nerves. He ought to take her soon and ease his hunger. She was ready. *Avida.*

Tomorrow he would suggest a trip to the sandy cove below the cliff. While Lio slept in the beach house at siesta time he would seduce her. From that moment on, they would stay close and Lio would have to acknowledge him, or be forced to keep his distance from Verity.

He closed his eyes, trying to visualise the future. Perhaps in a couple of weeks it would all be over. Lio would run to him for everything he needed. They would play football, paddle, sit in the small boat and exclaim over the jewel-coloured fish off the headland. Verity would go home.

Verity. His eyes snapped open in shock, reeling from a

sick sensation that suddenly gripped his abdomen in a vice. Sitting up, he tried to calm himself. At the moment, he felt alarmed at the thought of Verity leaving because they had unfinished business between them.

Once they'd made love, he reasoned, his obsession would fade—and then he'd probably be counting the days till she left.

Unless she went, he'd never be Lio's prime carer. It had to be. He would not accept being second-best in his son's eyes.

The nausea ebbed, the strong muscle contractions of his abdomen eased. With a sigh, he lay back again. And then those muscles—along with everything else in his body—tightened again in an instant as the door opened and Verity walked into his room.

He stifled a groan. This time she was naked.

She came to the bed, her eyes distant and unseeing. And he froze, silent and immobile but with all kinds of torment ripping through him.

The perfection of her body left him in awe. The sweet swell of her high, firm breasts. The alluring curve of her small waist. The flatness of her stomach and the dark triangle of hair that matched the jet cloud framing her lovely face.

He swallowed. Felt impelled to move when she gave a sigh and pulled back the sheet that covered him. Something held him there and he lay rigid, straining.

To his dismay, she sat on the bed and began to stroke his body; first his chest, tracing the shape of his ribs and muscles. Then his tightly-contracted stomach. Her fingers paused in their inexorable journey and he closed his eyes in agony. Expecting. Hoping. Knowing he should stop this—but how?

Gently, as if in wonder, she touched the swollen tip of him, that leapt to her fingers in an instant response. It was like a delicious torture. The merest caress of her questing forefinger was bringing him to the point of explosion.

Then abruptly she rose and left the room, stumbling against the door as she passed through it. When he heard her bump into one of the landing tables he slid, shaking, from the bed. She might do herself harm. Could fall down the stairs…

Grabbing his white silk robe, he also stumbled on his way to the door, his brain and body barely under control. At the last minute he had enough presence of mind to remember the baby monitor, which he pushed into the pocket of his robe before emerging on the landing.

Verity was already halfway down the stairs. Heart crashing in his ears, he went back for the sheet to cover her, intending to lead her back to her room. But now she was running, light as a feather, her hair streaming behind her as she sped unerringly across the hall and through the dining room to the terrace door.

Vittore dived for the house alarm and managed to turn it off before she wrenched at the handle. She moved like lightning, running across the terrace and down to the lawn before his aroused body could manage to cross half that distance.

He caught up with her in the lower garden. She lifted her head as though she could smell the angels' trumpets and raised her arms to the glittering sky. The scent of orange blossom drifted on the air from the orange grove above and fireflies pulsed in the grass.

Fireflies, he thought. Sending out mating signals to mates who might never come. In which case, the glow would become weaker and weaker over the next few nights until the fireflies died, their biological purpose unrealised.

Eyes dark with frustration, he watched Verity sink to the ground and stretch out as if in sacrifice, her beautiful body gleaming in the moonlight.

He had to get her back for her own safety. Quietly he knelt beside her and carefully slid a hand beneath her shoulders to raise her up.

'Vittore,' she whispered, startling him.

He couldn't breathe. Could not move. Her arms came around his neck and her naked body pressed against his, nestling to him until there was not a millimetre between them.

His head spun. He had never been so aroused in the whole of his life. He couldn't do anything other than tense every muscle while she sighed and whispered into his hot, pulsing throat as her hands sought another, fiercer pulse and rendered him helpless.

'No,' he breathed, though it was nothing more than an inaudible groan. 'Verity! *Ti desidero tantissimo!*' he moaned. 'But…come back to bed. Your bed. Alone!'

'Mmm!' she murmured, sliding down and taking him in her mouth.

And he was broken. All good intent, honour and pride vanished. She had taken him too far, further than any red-blooded male could ever withstand. He raised her head and kissed her with all the passion and fury in his fevered body.

She gasped and shuddered, speaking his name. Somewhere in the back of his mind he registered that she wasn't asleep after all. Her eyes were dark violet and bright, gazing at him in full recognition. Anger and then relief swept through him. She knew very well what she was doing—had lured him into the garden and deliberately enticed him!

Her breasts heaved against his chest in the sudden silence, the intensity of the night-scented flowers suddenly enhanced. All his senses were heightened, he realised, because he even heard the faint tinkle of the waterfall, far above, and the gurgle of the rill that fed it.

Verity's eyes closed, the thick lashes fluttering darkly. And he remained still and silent. It was important to him that she made the running. Then she could never claim that he had seduced her.

Willing, therefore, to let her take the initiative, he waited, intensely aware of a deep, internal bruising ache that he knew only she could relieve.

Gently she pushed him back and he made no resistance, his robe falling open. Her body lay on his. They kissed. No, that couldn't describe what they were doing. It was like no kissing he had ever known. It seemed they couldn't get enough of one another, their mouths gently savaging, tasting, sucking, whispering.

He tried to hold back, not to rush her. God knows, he tried. With a quick flip of his hands he rolled her over and began to kiss every inch of her, ignoring her little whimpers and cries, intent on making this the most perfect night she had ever experienced.

His mind was focussed just on pleasing her. On tasting the faint slick of sweat that slid between them, making their bodies move like liquid. Her frantic kisses and searching hands drove his needs deeper and deeper until every pore and vein and bone vibrated with the one compulsion to fill her with him and take her to the edge of sanity, where he already hovered.

'Are you sure you want this?' he whispered in a thick growl.

'Very,' she breathed.

'You are…safe?' he asked delicately.

She gave a wicked chuckle. 'Not in the least! Very, very dangerous!' she teased.

But she must have been protected because her hands guided him, faltering in their urgency. Wanting to thrust with violent relief, he somehow held on to some part of his conscious brain and eased into her warm softness gently, a little at a time, a slight withdrawal, a firmer drive…

'What do I do?' she breathed throatily in his ear. 'I want to move… Is that all right? Tell me. Teach me, Vittore!'

He went still. Raised himself a little his expression bewildered, unbelieving. Surely she didn't mean…

'Teach you?' he echoed dazedly.

Her hot eyes glowed. His heart swooped in response to

her beauty. 'I've never gone this far before,' she husked in little breathless jerks.

Hell. He closed his eyes. And, despite her pleas and clinging—then battering hands—he drew from the tightening spasms of her silken core and flung himself out on the ground beside her, his arms above his head gripping the grass as if he'd drown otherwise.

Her hand smoothed over his tightly clenched buttock. 'No!' he groaned, rolling away.

With shaking fingers he drew his robe around him and secured it tightly, keeping his back to her all the time.

'What are you playing at, Vittore?' she protested jerkily.

He had to stay detached or he'd fling decency to the four winds and make love to her.

'I'll see you back to your room,' he said, his tone hard and cold.

'What?' she cried, bewildered.

'You don't want to get pregnant, do you?' he asked coolly, turning to face her.

'N-no.' First she blushed and then her eyes went dreamy and sad.

For one mad moment he felt a lurch in his heart at the incredible thought of Verity carrying his baby within her. And then he dismissed it with a scowl and got to his feet, putting a healthier distance between them.

'Then we'd better go back.'

'Ohh!' she cried, her hand flying to her mouth. 'Is that what you meant when you asked if I was safe? I thought… I wasn't thinking. My brain wasn't functioning. You did that to me!' she accused.

He held out his hand politely. Crossly she took it and he pulled her up. Then he bent and picked up his sheet embroidered with violets the colour of her eyes and wrapped her in it till all he could see was her unhappy face.

'Let's go.'

'Not till you've explained yourself!' she cried furiously.

'What did you do? How did you get me out here? Why was I naked, with no clothes anywhere in sight? Was it the date rape drug? You louse!' she sobbed. 'Is that what you do to women?'

The shock made him reel. That she could think so badly of him was beyond belief.

His eyes glittered, black and sparking with unholy rage. 'If I want a woman,' he growled, 'I seduce her. I have no need of artificial aids!'

'So I decided to become a naturist without realising it?' she hurled jerkily.

'You're making excuses!' he grated. 'You were fully aware of what you were doing when you came into my room—'

'I did *what?*' she yelled, almost losing control of the sheet as she let it slip in her anger.

Now she was going to lie. Turn it all so that it was his fault. Well, he wasn't going to let her.

'You know damn well!' he roared. 'You drifted in, did a very good impression of a stripper and removed your nightdress.'

'You're making this up! I wouldn't do anything so outrageous!' she declared indignantly.

'Then how do you explain how you got here?'

'You...did something,' she said, clearly appalled at the depths he'd sink to.

'I will not have you suggesting that I'm some kind of pervert!' he seethed. 'I know what you were doing and what you did. You sat on my bed...' He swallowed. His voice had become croaky. And no wonder.

'What then?' she scathed. 'Did I suggest we might go for a walk?'

His mouth tightened. Despite his anger, his body was leaping with life, tormenting him with the memory.

'You touched me,' he said thickly.

'Oh, yes? Where?' she scorned.

His brows met in a terrible frown. 'Think of the most intimate part of the male anatomy.'

She looked in horror at her hands as if they had stroked him, not her lips. He didn't dare enlighten her.

'Now I know you're lying!' she cried, her face aflame. 'I—I wouldn't *dream* of doing what you said! How dare you suggest—?'

'I suppose you're going to pretend you were sleepwalking again,' he snapped cynically.

She froze. Looked at him in alarm. 'Again?' she whispered. 'What do you mean?'

'Oh, come on, Verity. You can't make out that you don't know. You must have woken in strange places and wondered how you'd got there.'

Her horror seemed genuine. 'I—I have,' she said in a small, scared voice. 'In England. Linda's house. I woke up one morning—not long before you arrived—and I was lying on the floor by Lio's cot.' She jiggled about in agitation. 'Do you think I was sleepwalking then? And…how do you know about it, anyway?' she demanded.

'Because several times you came to Lio's nursery while I slept there. You curled up on the floor and went to sleep. You usually went back to bed in the early hours.'

'What…' She gulped, her face a picture of dismay. 'What did you do?' she squeaked.

'Turned over and went to sleep, too,' he muttered. But didn't say that it had taken a hell of a time to do so. 'I can promise you, Verity,' he drawled, 'that if I had taken advantage of the situation and made love to you, you would have known about it.'

'Oh. I'm sorry. I—I honestly had no idea! Why didn't you say what I was doing?' she cried, aghast.

'I imagined it was stress because you were worried about Lio. I didn't see what could be done,' he said irritably. 'Short of tying you to your bedpost.'

That was a mistake. He'd had a quick vision of Verity complying with a sex game, her hands lightly caught by silk scarves, her eyes inviting him to plunder her eagerly defenceless body.

'Well,' she said breathily, 'that's what must have happened tonight—I was sleepwalking! But this time you clearly *did* take advantage of me, Vittore!'

'Like hell I did!' he snarled. 'And you can forget the sleepwalking excuse. I looked into your eyes and you were fully awake—'

'Yes, I did wake!' she cried helplessly. 'And found—found I was in your arms and you were t-touching me and—'

'And then you led me on,' he grated, wanting her, desperate to stop this argument and seal the matter once and for all.

'I'm inexperienced!' she protested. 'You must have already done goodness knows what to arouse me and I didn't know what was going on inside me. I don't have the defences or the sexual knowledge of a woman of the world,' she stormed. 'You knew that and—'

'I've had enough!' He held her shoulders and fixed her with a furious glare. 'I know what you did. If I hadn't mentioned the possibility of pregnancy, we would have made love. That's what you really want, isn't it? That's why you enticed me out here and pretended to be unaware of what you were doing—'

'I *was* unaware!' she sobbed, tears trickling from the corners of her watery violet eyes. 'You know I've been sleepwalking in the past. Why won't you accept that I might have been this time?'

'Because trust works both ways,' he said bitterly. 'And until we trust one another we can't ever be free of doubt and suspicion. I know you want me. I'm not stupid. I can understand why you want to salvage your pride by claiming that I used underhand means to get you out here. But you're not pinning this one on me. I operate by a code of honour—'

'Honour? You virtually said you wanted me as your whore!' she spat.

'Sure I want you. But not comatose!' he roared. He couldn't contain his anger as it boiled within him, firing his passion to dangerous heights. 'I want you to be willing,' he husked, seeing her eyes melt helplessly at his low, enraged growl. 'To hurl yourself at me, tearing at my clothes, groaning, moaning, begging me to hold you and caress you, to take away your ache and make love to you until you don't know if it's day or night and whether you are standing or sitting or sprawled defenceless on my bed! I know what we can be together. And I want you to be fully aware of every second of pleasure I give you because I will want you eager and waiting for me whenever we can be alone. And that will happen, Verity, because we can't stop it, nor do we want to.'

She was trembling, visibly shaken by his passionate outburst.

'You are very experienced and you know how to touch a woman and make her want you,' she mumbled through her tears. 'And it's not fair! What chance have I—?'

'None.'

He kissed her, somehow moved by her helplessness. His mouth took in all her tears, gently erasing them from her face and she moaned, biting her lip as she remained stiff and unyielding in his arms.

'Give in to it,' he coaxed, kissing her mouth into soft pliancy again.

'No!' she croaked. 'I'll do everything I can to keep you away! You are a sexual adventurer, Vittore, eager to move from woman to woman. I despise you for that. And also for using your expertise on an innocent like me, as a means to an end. You want to show Lio that we're in some kind of affectionate relationship, thinking that he'll show more interest in you. Well, I won't be used! I won't! So get used to the idea of losing your bet! After what you did tonight, I'm convinced that you're not worthy to be his father! And

I hope to heaven I can protect him from your vile influence!'

Weeping uncontrollably, she tore from his grasp and began to stumble towards the house, fumbling occasionally with the sheet which seemed intent on unravelling and tripping her up.

Vittore kept a wise yard or two behind and only moved closer when he saw that she had crumpled into a heap at the foot of a flight of stone steps and seemed to be sobbing her heart out.

'Verity—'

'Don't touch me!' she yelled. 'I can manage. It's this wretched sheet. I'm all tangled up—and—and I w-want this nightmare to end and to be back in bed and for it all to have been a horrible *dream*!'

Heaving a heavy sigh, he saw only one way out. He picked her up, ignoring her fists thumping against his chest, ignoring too the fact that her action had made the sheet expose more of her body than he would have wished to see.

Grimly he strode to the house while she threatened him with hell and damnation if he laid a finger on her. With cold deliberation he tipped her on her bed.

He bent low and kissed her fiercely until she began to unwind her taut limbs and they wrapped themselves around him. Viciously controlling himself, he waited until she was returning his kisses with frantic eagerness and then he whispered in her ear.

'I could make love to you now,' he said softly. 'But I won't, because that would be taking advantage of you. Is that the action of a man who means to have you and doesn't care how he does?'

She froze. He stalked out, closing the door with an unnecessarily hard slam.

He'd make her come to him, he thought, shaking with rage. And she'd apologise for suggesting he might have acted dishonourably.

A week, he vowed. That's how long it would take.

CHAPTER NINE

ALONE in her room, Verity tried to turn herself from wanton hussy into the sexless person she'd been before she'd met Vittore.

In vain she tried to drag air into her lungs, to make her body rigid instead of the consistency of jelly, to clear her head of the battling emotions; anger and desire.

She groaned, passing a shaking hand over her sweating forehead. How could she ever risk going to sleep again? Her unconscious mind might take over, she thought gloomily. She'd go into sleepwalking mode and appear in Vittore's bedroom wearing nothing but a come-hither smile and proceed to humiliate herself again.

Her hands covered her face in shame and she screwed her body up small as if to make it disappear. She couldn't understand why she weakened every time Vittore touched her. Normally she was so strong-willed. With him, she had the strength of limp celery.

Oh, this was awful! She had to think rationally. To work out where his interests lay. Then she might be able to understand his intentions.

Tense and agitated, she jumped up and dressed in her old clothes and went downstairs to sit on the terrace. The cool night air soothed her fevered brow and her hectic breathing became calmer.

Vittore, she reasoned, wanted Lio as soon as possible. His best way to achieve that would be—as she'd already thought—to have some kind of affectionate relationship with her. So she'd be mad ever to trust him by offering her virginity.

Of course it was perfectly possible that his interest might

be sexual *as well.* What red-blooded man would turn down the chance to make love to a willing woman, provided she was below the age of seventy and had her own teeth and hair? And Vittore had more red blood than most…

He had only drawn back when he'd realised they might make a baby. Her mouth thinned. That must have been a shock! Before that moment he'd thought he had her on a plate—and that Lio would soon warm to him.

But now she had to close her mind and body to Vittore. To care for Lio and keep him from harm. And do whatever was best for her darling baby.

Perhaps because of the tense atmosphere between herself and Vittore, Lio seemed unusually clinging the next day.

And, having been up half the night, Verity's reserves of patience were lower than normal. On the beach below the house, she tried to be bright and perky for her nephew but it was hard with Vittore oozing charisma a few feet away and displaying his magnificent body in a brief pair of shorts.

Casually he emerged from the beach house carrying a foot pump and proceeded to inflate a small boat. Without comment, he clambered into it and began paddling around the shallows of the cobalt sea.

''Ook!' exclaimed Lio enviously.

'Boat,' she said, thinking what fun it looked.

Enviously she shaded her eyes and gazed at the lazily reclining Vittore, whose eyes were masked by sunglasses.

'Papa,' Lio said suddenly.

Verity froze. 'Papa,' she breathed, her heart going crazy.

'Papa.' Lio beamed and she didn't know whether to laugh or cry.

Emotion filled her up. It was coming, she thought; Lio's reliance on her would fade and be directed towards his father. The most natural thing in the world. They'd play boy's games like football, kicking with the side of the foot instead of their toes as she did. Lio would squeal with delight as he was hurled about in the air and then deposited on his father's broad shoulders. She could hardly breathe. Her beloved Lio would become a stranger she visited a couple of times a year.

The pain seared her chest. With watery eyes, she fumbled her way to her feet and walked down to the water's edge.

'He said "Papa",' she announced flatly.

The sunglasses were whipped off. 'What?'

'You heard.' Oh, she thought, that was ungracious. But it hurt so much!

'Verity!' He leapt out, unusually graceless, landing in the water with a splash. She heard Lio laugh and clap behind her and the ache in her heart grew fiercer. Vittore found his feet and came to her, his eyes bright with joy. 'Say it. Tell me again!' he breathed.

Her mouth wobbled horribly. 'He—said—"Papa",' she parroted.

She could feel Vittore's tension, could see the heart-rending relief in his expressive face and body.

He stepped to one side and looked down. She realised that Lio was inches away from her, his foreign legion hat askew on his blond head, deep blue eyes bright within their fringe of black lashes.

Shaking, Vittore held out his hand to his son. 'Lio! Come in the boat with Papa,' he coaxed, an assumed jollity only just concealing his elation.

Lio continued to stare. Vittore crouched down, a look of such pure love on his face that Verity actually willed Lio to accept his father's hand. But she kept quiet, knowing that any word from her might remind Lio that he normally clung to her like moss to stone.

'Veevee,' Lio said in panic, reaching his arms high to Verity.

'You go with Papa in the boat,' she encouraged shakily.

'No! Veevee!' Lio's face crumpled.

'It's OK. You take him,' croaked Vittore.

She glanced at him, appalled by the utter misery in his voice. He didn't look at her but rose and strode back up the beach, gathering his things and then heading up the path to the house, his entire body displaying a terrible dejection.

She sought him out later, when Lio slept after lunch, the baby alarm safely in her pocket. A worried-looking Maria, brutally kneading bread on the thick marble counter in the kitchen, directed her eventually to the salon.

Tentatively Verity opened the double doors. He sat by the open window, slumped on a huge sofa, his head in his hands. And she felt desperately sorry for him even though she should be glad that Lio was still a long way from accepting his father.

She didn't know what to do. Couldn't fathom why she minded so much that he was so hurt by his son's rejection. She despised Vittore, didn't she? Her attitude made no sense at all.

'Vittore,' she said hesitantly.

'Come to gloat?' he growled.

'No.' He mustn't think that. Quickly she padded in her bare feet across the cool marble floor, a long scarlet shirt concealing her white bikini. 'I wanted him to acknowledge you,' she told him shakily. 'I wanted him to play in the boat with you. Don't ask me why, because I don't know myself. Only that I can't bear to see him rejecting you any more.'

His brooding eyes flicked up to hers and then his lashes had lowered to hide his reaction.

'I don't know what to do,' he muttered. 'It's tearing me apart.' He flashed her an angry look then. 'The whole damn thing about the two of you is destroying me!' he rasped.

She made to place a sympathetic hand on his shoulder. 'I'm sorry—'

'Don't touch me!' he growled irritably and leapt up to stand in front of the window with his back to her, his shoulders high with tension. 'You think I took advantage of you. I can't tell you how that makes me feel. And I don't know how I can convince you that I believed you knew what you were doing—and that I would have coaxed you back to bed if I'd truly thought you were sleepwalking.'

She hung her head. 'I daren't trust you,' she whispered. 'Your reputation—'

'I don't have one!' he snapped, spinning around to face her. 'Except for honesty and honour! Don't you know that I have been celibate ever since Lio was conceived? That I have paid for my mistake with Linda a thousand times and have shunned women as a result?'

'Bianca—' she began jerkily.

'Bianca? She was the one who listened to my anguish, who plied me with coffee and sat up all night quietly holding my hand and keeping me sane!' he muttered. 'Ask my mother. She was there for me too. I love Bianca as a sister. But I've never felt passion for her, not even when she held me in her arms when I despaired of ever finding my son.'

'You were engaged,' she persisted.

'No. It was assumed we'd get engaged. Bianca and I knew that would never happen. Why,' he flung suddenly, 'do you think I am so consumed with hunger for you? It's because no woman has ever aroused me as much as you do—and because I have not been touched sexually for over two years and my blood beats hot and fast in my body every time you're near!'

'I—I can't help that! What can I do?' she cried, shocked by his fervour. Could that be true? If only…

'Do? You could wear a refuse bag instead of that revealing wrap,' he snarled and strode angrily out of the room.

She didn't know whether to smile or weep. So after checking that Lio still slept soundly, she went into the garden, hoping that its serenity would calm her down. She needed to think.

'What a terrible mood Vittore's in!' exclaimed Honesty, appearing from behind a dark yew which she'd clearly been clipping into the shape of a manic-looking hedgehog.

Verity sighed. So much for thinking time. But perhaps this would be the opportunity she wanted to learn a little more about Vittore.

So she wandered over to Vittore's mother, anxious to ask the questions that burned in her mind.

'I expect he's bothered about Lio,' she replied as a starter. 'He dearly wants to cuddle him.'

'I know. I'm desperate too and I'm only his grandmother. I ache every time I see my grandson. I want to hold that little body and hug him tight.' Honesty groaned extravagantly. 'It must be doubly hard for Vittore, when he was such a devoted father.'

And with that, she absently snipped off the tip of the hedgehog's nose, making him look even odder.

'He wasn't away on business trips then?' Verity probed.

'No!' The pruners were waved about dangerously and Verity ducked. 'He hardly left Lio's side. He fitted in his work at night, when Lio slept. Tore realised that his son wasn't going to get much cuddling from Linda,' Honesty mused. 'I don't think she knew how to be a mother. Abdicated her responsibilities as fast as she could and started going out to clubs.'

Vittore's mother began to dead-head roses and Verity helped, her pulses racing.

'That must have upset him,' she ventured, trying to keep her voice even.

'Not really. I think he was relieved to be shot of her. It was a mistake to have married her,' Honesty said sternly. 'I told him at the time, but he would do the right thing. These Italians! Their honour and family name is of the utmost importance. Pick those lily beetles off, will you? I told him, if you don't love her, if she's threatening to abort her child—'

'What?' Verity gasped, frozen with horror.

'Oh, it was the way Linda got him where she wanted him,' Honesty said cynically. 'She coveted his wealth and made a play. I scolded him for not using a contraceptive,' she declared, making Verity blush at Honesty's frankness. 'But he said that Linda had told him she was on the pill. I knew then that this abortion thing was a ploy to land him. He couldn't bear the thought of a child of his being killed. So they got married and his hell began.'

'A...bortion?' Verity whispered in horror.

'I loathed the woman from then on.' Honesty started savaging the roses in her righteous anger and a beautiful Fantin-Latour would have had its height cut from six to two feet, if Verity hadn't intervened. 'How could she use her unborn child as a means to an end?'

Verity suddenly felt awful, probing into Vittore's private affairs. She had no right. Except that she needed to know. Already she'd learnt more than she had wanted to hear. Linda was as bad as she'd feared. No wonder Lio had been thin and hungry and confused, if she was as bad a mother as Honesty had said.

'Vittore must have needed comfort when his marriage failed,' she said slowly. 'It's times like that when men turn to other women—'

'Vittore?' Honesty snorted. 'He'd had his fingers bitten. He wasn't going to stick them in the honey again. No. He just flung all his love at Lio, talked to me and Bianca about how he felt and did his best to keep the marriage going. He was always polite to Linda. Said she was the mother of his child and deserved that, at least. But I didn't find it easy to be nice to her, I can tell you!'

A drift of cosmos received Honesty's ruthless attentions. Verity wondered how the garden survived her attacks, though she recognised that she was upset about her son and that pruning and chopping was her therapy.

'No infidelity on Vittore's part, then.'

She needed to be sure. Though...what did a mother know about her children's relationships? She bit her lip.

'Huh. Infidelity. He wouldn't stoop so low. He sees marriage as a sacrament. Pity Linda didn't feel the same. There's a Neapolitan saying. ''Toothbrushes and wives are not for sharing.'' Linda needed attention and love and admiration, you see, and she wasn't getting it from Vittore. So she looked elsewhere. It was awful,' Honesty said with a sniff, 'seeing my son so miserable—and so horribly helpless!'

'It must have been. How did he find out?' Verity asked, gently placing her hand over the woman's shaking fingers.

Honesty turned to her, the bright eyes dull with misery. 'In the worst possible way, Verity!' she said helplessly. 'Lio had a fever. One of those childhood things. The doctor came and Vittore spent all night sponging Lio down as he'd been instructed. In the morning when the fever had gone and Lio slept, Vittore went looking for Linda in a towering rage. He found her in a squalid little rental apartment with two drunken tourists. I won't go into details. Vittore came back as white as a sheet. And that was it. My heart bled for him. He told her that he wanted a divorce.'

'But…why did Linda run away, when she could have had half his fortune?' Verity asked, ashamed to be linked with Linda, even by adoption.

'I don't know,' replied Honesty. 'She just disappeared off the face of the earth. And from that moment, Vittore grieved as though his life had ended. It was touching that the people in the village prayed for him. They are so fond of him,' she said gently, tears blurring her eyes. 'Maria made his favourite meals and he tried hard to eat them to please her.' She sighed. 'Everyone cares for my son. He is respected and loved by all who know him and I am so proud of him. It broke our hearts that he lost interest in life and became so thin and gaunt.' Honesty snuffled into a handkerchief. 'It was only Bianca who forced him to think of others by showing him pictures of sick children and reminding him that he still had more than others. It hurts me now to see him watching Lio and not being able to sweep his baby up in his arms and enjoy him as he used to. He deserves better. I can't bear it, Verity,' she sobbed. 'I just can't bear it!'

She took Vittore's mother in her arms and hugged her, shedding tears herself. It seemed she might have been wrong. Again. Even taking into account the fact that every mother thought her child was a swan, there was no mistaking the truth of Honesty's words, or the unusual concern and affection shown by the villagers.

'Help him!' pleaded Honesty, clutching Verity tightly. 'Lio needs his father and Vittore needs his son!' she cried plaintively.

Verity swallowed. 'I know,' she said in a husky whisper.

The trouble was, she thought unhappily, she needed them both, too.

Her head lifted. Lio was stirring. 'I must go,' she said gently.

''Course.' Honesty dashed the back of her grubby hands across her eyes, leaving streaks of dirt. 'Do what you can,' she said in a small voice.

Touched by the dramatic change from a confident, enthusiastic woman to someone so deeply unhappy for her beloved son, Verity hugged Vittore's mother and kissed her tear-stained cheek.

'I'll…try,' she promised shakily.

And hurried to collect Lio and bring him down to the garden to play. Reeling from what Honesty had told her, Verity tried to put her mind to entertaining the fractious little boy just as Vittore came striding across the lawn, his face dark and brooding.

Lio took one look and flung himself into her arms. That set the pattern for the rest of the day, which was a disaster. By the evening she was at screaming point. Lio had indulged in two tantrums and deliberately banged his head on the ground in his paddy. Vittore had remained in the background, saying nothing.

But she could feel his distress, his helplessness. And wanted to weep.

It was very late by the time she had finally settled Lio for the night. To her dismay, Vittore was waiting outside the nursery door. She frowned, wishing she could have had time to consider what Honesty had said. To rethink her position.

But seeing Vittore put all thought to flight. He had changed into a cream summer suit and powder blue shirt for dinner, his freshly shaven face as smooth as satin and offering her tantalising drifts of his exclusive aftershave.

'What?' she asked grumpily, too weary to be civil.

'You've had a tough day.'

'Nothing unusual.'

'I'm sorry, Verity. I apologise for my bad temper. I felt so helpless.'

His voice sounded like rippling silk, so musical and invasive that it was easing her tense muscles and furrowed brow without effort. She didn't look at him. Couldn't.

'I do understand,' she said huskily. 'The pain of not holding your child and watching him from afar must be sheer hell.' Then she did look up, and trembled at the tenderness in his dark eyes. 'I'd be far worse in your place,' she babbled. 'China would get smashed. I'd eat carpets. Rip up telephone directories.'

A smile touched his wan lips. 'Thank you. Always ready with something to lift my spirits.'

Oh, yes, she thought. Star comedienne, she was. But she wanted to weep for him. And then she'd cry for Lio and then herself and Honesty. They were all in a pit of darkness.

'Is he asleep?' he murmured.

She heaved a heavy sigh. 'Yes.'

'Good. When you've changed, get a blanket and bring him to the hall.'

Her eyes widened at the unexpected order. He'd already started towards the stairs as if he expected her to obey!

'I don't think so!' she muttered in automatic protest.

He froze. Turned, came slowly towards her again, his eyes dark and piercing.

'You will do this, Verity,' he said softly. But the silk barely covered the steel beneath. 'If you won't, then I will go in and get him,' he said evenly.

'This is your son!' she cried, indignantly, deciding that maybe she wouldn't weep for him after all. 'You can't haul him about like a piece of luggage—'

'This is a special occasion. There's a party in the village. A surprise party,' he explained, still reasonable, still determined that she should obey him. 'The villagers have spent all day preparing for it—'

'Well they don't need Lio or me there!' she argued.

'It's *for* him.'

She blinked. 'But it's not his birthday!'

'It might as well be.' Vittore's expression gentled. The sadness of his smile ate into her heart. 'You see, Verity, they are thrilled that he's back with me. They've gone to a great deal of effort. Maria reports that there are tables set up in the square and along the streets, balloons, fireworks planned—'

'But...Lio can't possibly go—!'

'They all know that he's wary of strangers,' Vittore explained. 'That is why they timed it for this evening, so that he would be sleeping. They want to see him and thought this would be the best way to save him from any distress.'

She stared at him, touched by the villagers' interest. But exasperated, too.

'It's just not on! You know it isn't,' she said firmly. 'If he wakes—'

'Don't make problems that don't exist.' He frowned at her reprovingly. 'He sleeps well at night. If he stirs you always settle him down again. But, as a precaution, I want you to come too. If you refuse to come then I'll take him myself. He's going, whatever you decide.'

Her body slumped. 'But...I'm so tired—'

'Please yourself.' Calm and polite, he moved towards the nursery door.

'No!' She bit her lip. 'You've done it again,' she complained. 'You put me in an impossible situation!' Irritated by his manipulation, she added, 'Aren't these villagers a bit arrogant to imagine they can organise a party and expect you to drag your toddler out of bed for it?'

'You don't understand,' he said softly. 'Let me explain. When Lio disappeared, they were all distressed. They sent letters, flowers, little gifts of sympathy. They knew Lio. They'd celebrated his birth here in the house and Lio was passed from hand to loving hand. They adored him. Whenever we went into the village he was surrounded by admirers. The carpenter made his crib and several toys. Women embroidered clothes for him, schoolchildren tickled him under his chin and competed to make him laugh. Their affection and kindness means a great deal to me. Maria told them that he sleeps soundly and would not be disturbed,' he said, his eyes dark and warm with affection for the people of his village. 'Verity,' he coaxed, 'they are anxious to celebrate his return. And I am not going to disappoint them.'

Her head lowered in defeat. This fitted with what his mother had said. There was a special relationship between Vittore and the villagers. And against such compelling arguments, how could she refuse?

'Of course. I didn't realise. I just wanted to protect him,' she said in a small voice.

He beamed, dazzling her. 'I know,' he said softly.

She gulped. 'I'll shower and change. Then I'll get him.'

They walked to her bedroom door and he opened it politely. When it shut behind her, she stopped and closed her eyes, trying to draw in strength for the evening ahead. And then she hurried to find something to wear.

In a simple white cotton dress, its scoop neck and full skirt flattering her figure more than she remembered, she felt she looked good, at least. Hastily she grabbed hanks of hair and pinned them up on top of her head then dashed a slash of lipstick across her mouth.

Her eyes seemed huge and startled, sparkling with nervous anticipation. There was a hectic colour in her cheeks. She stared at herself in dismay, knowing that her suppressed excitement was all to do with spending the evening close to Vittore, and not because of the party.

But they would be chaperoned, she reminded herself. By a few hundred people. Fortified by that thought, she walked boldly out. And immediately faltered, shaken by Vittore's stunned reaction.

'You look very beautiful,' he said huskily.

She swallowed, devastated by the sultriness of his mouth and the admiration in his eyes.

'The dress cost two pounds fifty in the Portobello Road,' she announced hastily and escaped to the nursery, thanking the Fates for her quick tongue. She had almost simpered and said breathlessly, 'Do I?' in which case he would have known he was home and dry as far as his seduction plans were concerned.

Briskly she collected a blanket and tucked it around Lio then lifted him into her arms.

'Right. We're ready,' she said. 'You bring his changing bag, just in case.'

He slung it on his shoulder and, contrary to her hopes, it didn't detract from his sexy image one bit. He must have been raking a hand through his hair while she changed, because that Byron lick had fallen onto his forehead, giving him extra sex-appeal.

And when he took her elbow the warmth of his cupped hand transmitted itself to her and with it came all the familiar surges of tension rippling through her veins.

'I appreciate this,' he confided. 'I know you're tired. I'll stay with you and keep an eye on you—'

'I'll be fine on my own,' she muttered nervously.

'I think I'll have to. I'd better warn you now. They'll

be wary of you to begin with,' he explained as they walked down the stairs together.

Her brow furrowed and she flung him a puzzled glance. 'Me? Why?'

'Because you are Linda's sister.'

She thought for a moment. 'They didn't like her?' she ventured. Her heart beat rapidly. No one seemed to like Linda. Was that why she left, because she felt unwelcome?

Vittore had remained silent, his face dark and stormy as if unpleasant memories were filling his head.

'No,' he said eventually.

'Well, I'm not my sister,' she pointed out.

'Far from it. But there could be some awkward moments,' he mused. 'We must make it clear that Mother and I are convinced you are good for Lio.'

'How do you propose doing that?'

He shrugged. 'I thought we could smile a lot at one another. Look friendly.'

'Not a good idea,' she said flatly.

She knew his version of 'friendly'. It involved a lot of touching. And she wasn't going to spend another sleepless night tussling with her wish that he would pounce and be done with it.

Vittore heaved a heavy sigh. 'I thought you cared about Lio?' he reproached, bending his head to her in a gesture that assailed her senses with gleaming honey skin, smoke-black eyes and a hint of expensive soap.

'I do,' she said shortly, having trouble stiffening her watery knees.

'Then surely you realise,' he argued with infuriatingly calm reasoning, 'that if he is to integrate with the people in the village then it won't help if there's a bad atmosphere every time you turn up with him. I realise it will be in your interest for my son to feel he is a stranger in his own home, but—'

'No,' she denied. 'I wouldn't want that. I don't want

him upset. My dearest wish is that he feels happy and relaxed with people.'

'Then do your part,' Vittore urged.

'But...I don't want to cosy up to you! Can't I keep patting his head and tucking in his blanket? Or—?'

'Your feelings aren't important tonight.' Dark eyes serious, he paused by the front door, his eyes glittering in the artificial light from the huge crystal chandelier. 'Don't mistake what I am doing. This is not for you. These are good, honest people, Verity. They want the fairy tale to be true and I'm not going to let them down. The heir to the Mantezzini estates has returned and in time he will grow up under the loving and watchful eyes of everyone here.'

'You can't be sure of that,' she said quietly, anxious that his hopes weren't raised too high. 'You must remember that he might be coming home with me.'

'True. But for tonight,' he replied, 'I want you to think of these people with good hearts, who believe in the happy ever after. I care about them, Verity. We are indivisible, the villagers, Lio and me. These people are part of his destiny. This land is his—and will belong to his children and his children's children. I don't expect you to understand. It isn't that I *own* the land—'

'You have it as a privilege,' she said thoughtfully, moved by his passion. 'And owe a duty to everyone on it.'

His eyebrow lifted a fraction. 'Exactly. I am impressed, Verity. You value Lio's heritage.'

He strode off to collect the buggy while she bit her lip, realising he'd backed her into a corner. But his description of Lio's place in this small and intimate world had been a revelation.

She contrasted it to the life Lio would lead with her in England. And found it wanting. No family. No loving community. Just her.

She felt a shiver of apprehension trickling down her back. Lio shouldn't be deprived of his birthright. For his sake she'd have to work hard to encourage Lio to love his father.

She began to tremble. It also meant that she'd be working towards her own hell.

No Vittore. No Lio. The bleakest future she could imagine.

CHAPTER TEN

DESPAIR wrenched at her heart. Her arms tightened around Lio, her gaze sightless and pained. She couldn't bear the thought of leaving either of them. But almost certainly that was what would happen.

Vittore returned and held the main door open for her. Like a zombie she walked out into the night.

Turning, she watched him coming down the steps; urbane, sophisticated, devastatingly handsome. Her stomach flipped as a matter of course and she merely accepted that that was what it did. It was too common an occurrence now to surprise her any more.

Helping her to tuck Lio into the buggy, he put a hand on her arm and asked softly, 'What about it, Verity? Will you co-operate?'

'Do you ever leave me with a choice?' she asked in an undertone.

She thought his face cracked into a faint smile but it was too fleeting to be sure.

'Thank you,' he said, his voice husky with warm gratitude. 'I am grateful. Ah. Here's Mother.'

With Lio in his buggy, they walked down to the village with Honesty, who chatted in her usual cheerful way, absolving her of any need to make conversation at all. Behind them, at a slower pace, came Maria and the valet, dressed in their Sunday best.

Even some distance away they heard the music drifting up and the sound of laughter. Verity took a deep breath just as Vittore's arm came around her shoulders.

'All right?' he murmured.

'Nervous. I've no idea why,' she muttered.

'Perhaps you are anxious that they should like you.'

'Can't think why.'

'No?' He grinned and she thought he seemed remarkably cheerful for a man whose son didn't want him. 'They'll love you,' he said. 'Here we are. Smile. It's the welcoming committee.'

It was like being admitted into a mother's arms. Not that she knew what *that* felt like. With that protective arm around her, Vittore beamed down at her as if she represented the world to him and she wished that she did.

The villagers responded to his approval as he'd predicted, kissing and hugging her, thanking her for bringing their *piccolino padrone* back to them all. And then they were swept triumphantly down the *vicoletti*, the stepped streets, and into the square.

'They want us to dance,' Vittore murmured in her ear.

She looked at him in alarm. The small square looked very festive; brightly lit by swinging hurricane lanterns and decked with streamers from one side to the other. In the middle sat a sweating band, who'd been playing fast and furious tunes up to now, but had unfairly switched to something that sounded unnervingly dreamy.

'In a minute,' she promised in panic. It was bad enough having Vittore's arm around her, let alone—

'Now.'

'But Lio—!' Her gasped protest was cut off abruptly.

'You can watch the buggy from the dance floor. They won't let him come to harm. One squeak and he'll be in your arms. A squeak from Lio, that is,' Vittore said drily.

'But—'

Smiling faces surrounded her. They were so nice, these people. So open in their joy for Lio. How could she be churlish?

Vittore sensed her surrender and led her onto the dance floor. A burst of clapping rang out, embarrassing her.

'I'm not very good,' she whispered.

'I'll lead you,' he husked in her ear.

She trembled. That was what she was afraid of. Even more than before, she had to keep her distance from Vittore. Then she wouldn't be hurt so badly when she left.

A tremor ripped through her. Panic created havoc in her stomach. She didn't want to leave, she thought miserably.

'Verity?'

'Right,' she said breathily, very erect, very rigid. His body was too close. A foot away—and she could feel his heat and the overpowering frisson that seemed to fill the air between them. 'Here we go,' she cried, trying to sound jaunty. 'Prepare for bruised toes. Smashed kneecaps. Cracked shins—'

'Relax,' he husked. 'You look as if you're ready for the firing squad.'

'That would be an improvement on this,' she muttered. Nevertheless, she did a cheesy grin for appearance's sake and lessened the distance between them a fraction.

He chuckled. 'Close your eyes and think of England.'

Her gaze flicked up to his in wry amusement. 'No woman with any sense would close her eyes when you're flinging charm and charisma around.'

He laughed, the sudden exposure of his gleaming teeth and satin throat, coupled with his evident delight, just made her feel weak and helpless. And before she knew it, she had been drawn against his wonderfully male chest and knew she was exactly where her body wanted her to be.

'Eyes open?' he queried, whirling her around until she felt even giddier and more disorientated than before.

'You bet,' she muttered into his shoulder.

Though only just. They kept wanting to close in bliss. Idly she wondered how she'd come to rest her head there.

The music became even more sultry. A tenor voice rang out and everyone turned to exclaim and clap.

Astonished, she saw an unusually tall man aged around seventy and with less teeth than must be comfortable, standing in front of the band. The sound that came from his mouth was like liquid gold and he sang the love song as though he were twenty and in love for the first time.

'Oh, it's lovely,' she whispered helplessly.

Vittore merely held her. But they were both moving more dreamily and she could feel her heart and her defences weakening.

'Don't get the wrong idea. I'm doing this for show,' she reminded him. And herself.

'Of course. What else?' he asked, all innocence.

Because I'm crazy about you, she thought helplessly. I hate it and resent it but can't stop myself from wanting to be with you. And when you laugh at the things I say, I am desperately flattered and delighted. I am infatuated with you. And nothing seems to kill my stupid admiration, not even the knowledge that I'm totally expendable. A temporary necessity.

'This is wonderful,' he murmured, his voice shaking with emotion.

'Kind of them to throw a party,' she agreed in a slurred mumble.

'It's good to be with people you love,' he husked.

'Yes,' she whispered, aghast.

Was that it? Had she fallen for him? Please, no! He wasn't the kind of man she'd imagined in that role. Too glorious a male to ever love her. Not second-hand-clothes-Verity. He'd break her heart…

He held her more tightly and she, foolish and unwise, clung to him as if she might drown otherwise. The love song soared and she heard agony and unrequited passion and then joy in the tenor's voice as he lived the emotions of the music.

Longing and desire vibrated from every note. And her body—quite independent of her own will—had responded to the siren call and now lay melting in Vittore's enclosing arms.

Her thigh moved with his. His hand splayed against her lower spine, fingers just invading the soft rise of her buttocks. And so her pelvis was thrust against his, the hardness of his arousal hot and demanding.

'Too friendly,' she grated in his ear.

'Convincing, though,' he breathed.

'Then if we've done our share of convincing, we can stop. Circulate.' As if her blood wasn't circulating like a raging torrent already! she thought ruefully. 'I think I ought to dance with the butcher first,' she jerked.

'His wife would be furious. Might take a carving knife to you and turn you into chops,' murmured Vittore.

The warm laughter in his voice wandered seductively through her flesh and bones and turned them to water.

'Please!' she whispered. 'Move back. You don't have to impress them with your Casanova techniques. They're staring at us,' she complained.

'Are they?' He looked around and grinned at several people before returning his attention to her. 'I've got used to it. Not much happens that they don't know about.'

'You have them in the palm of your hand. They respect you. Love you,' she said, resenting the success of his charm.

'I try to earn their respect,' he said quietly.

She turned her head and looked up at him. The villagers thought he was a good man. He was deeply admired by people who knew him well. Only she was holding out and any moment now she'd be worshipping him too.

'You have it. In spades,' she mumbled and heaved a sigh that made her entire body tremble.

Vittore's muscles tensed. The pressure against her pelvis burned hot and insistent.

'I think,' he said tightly, 'that you're right. I should circulate. What would *you* like to do?'

A little lost, definitely disappointed, she kept her face bright and tried valiantly to count her blessings that she wouldn't have to battle with her unhealthy desires. Or his.

'I'd like a cool drink, please,' she replied.

'I hope they've got ice,' he muttered.

She smiled faintly, flattered that she could arouse him so easily. They broke apart and he led her to where his mother sat, chatting to a group of villagers who leapt to their feet, applauded her and scrambled to be the one who offered her a chair.

Blushing from so much attention, she sat down and sipped the lemon drink she was offered. Everyone seemed to be talking at once; animated, excited, full of life and enthusiasm. Tiny children, still awake unlike Lio, were being passed around and admired, their squeals and laughter looked on benignly.

She loved Italians. Loved the way they expressed their feelings so readily—pushy, vocal, but never aggressive. She'd always felt so safe here, perhaps because Vittore had told her that no Italian male would ever hassle a woman with a child and she would be respected as a matter of course.

Coloured lights had been strung down the street that led to the harbour. Some of the palms were floodlit, giving the piazetta an exotic air. The town was in festive mood and everybody seemed determined to enjoy themselves until the early hours.

'It's a wonderful party,' she ventured to Honesty who was wearing a stunning beaded shawl in a startling kingfisher blue that competed violently with the orange hibiscus in her hair.

'Great people, aren't they?' she replied. 'Of course, Italians feel strongly about family. It's the most important thing in their lives. You can understand now how devastated they were when Linda snatched Lio—'

There was a dramatic chorus of disapproval and Verity realised the people around the table had caught Linda's name.

'See what I mean?' continued Honesty. 'They hated her for what she was doing to the honour of the family and the village. They knew what she was up to even though Vittore remained steadfast and wouldn't hear a word said against her. But she didn't realise that our lives are an open book here. The village looks after its own. Have some more lemon. Dear people.'

Honesty patted a woman's hand affectionately and nodded at the torrent of liquid Italian that followed.

'What did she say?' queried Verity, intrigued by the passionate waving of hands and the nods from their companions.

'That you are different. *Simpatico*,' she said, passing a plate of pastries towards Verity. 'They've cared for Vittore ever since he was old enough to totter down the hill,' she continued. 'They know him through and through and would trust him with their lives. Which is why they have gone to all this trouble. Excuse me,' she said, when Verity was intending to probe further when she'd finished the little tube of ricotta and sugar. 'I'm off to dance with the tax inspector. He does a wicked tango.'

Absorbing this further proof of Vittore's decency, Verity settled in her seat, nibbling the delicious pastries and sipping her drink as she watched Honesty and the tax inspector fling themselves whole-heartedly into an energetic tango that left Verity feeling breathless.

She watched Vittore carefully. He displayed the kind of old-fashioned good manners that she admired, talking easily and naturally to everyone there. The priest seemed to be an old friend and the two men spent a while together, apparently exchanging amusing stories because there was much laughter and slapping of backs between them.

The perfect man, she thought wistfully. And he returned frequently to her table, joking, smiling, touching her affectionately on the arm. Once or twice they danced together and fierce charges of electricity powered her body so that she didn't feel tired any more.

Falling more and more deeply in love with him, she drank more of the *limoncello* and felt heady with the music and laughter and dancing, until Vittore stayed her hand as she reached for the chilled jug to refill her glass.

'Verity,' he said throatily. 'You know this is made from lemon and sugar and vodka?'

Her eyes widened. 'No!' Her hand went to her head. It seemed definitely fluffy inside there. 'I think I'm a bit squiffy,' she complained.

'Perhaps it's time to get you and Lio back. The walk will sober you up,' he murmured. 'Come with me and we'll go around thanking everyone. They'll understand if I explain that you're tired from looking after Lio all day. Then we'll rescue him from the admirers clustered around him and make our way home.'

His arm enclosed her. She felt cherished. The smiles and affection of the villagers warmed her heart. This was a wonderful place, she thought dreamily. Lio would be cared for, here.

She imagined him 'tottering down to the village', totally safe because of those who would keep a loving eye on him. There would be a *gelato* from the ice-cream shop, pastries from the baker, a fruit drink from the *trattoria.*

Heavens! She'd have to regulate the treats. He'd be the size of a house by the time he reached fourteen!

But of course, she wouldn't be here. Someone else would have to keep an eye on his forays into the village.

Her lower lip wobbled. Her eyes became bleary. She wanted to see him blossom and grow. To watch him ride his first bike. To wave goodbye when he first went to school, to mop up bloody knees, and spaghetti from his shirt, to meet his first love and to be a part of his life, day by day.

The chances of that were now remote, she recognised that. She would be the maiden aunt who came over and asked him embarrassing questions when he wanted to be out with his friends. There would never be the deep love between them that she had originally anticipated with such joy and delight.

There would be hugs, maybe polite kisses. But never

that full-blown rush-at-you, fling your dirty self wildly into your mother's arms kind of moment.

Oh, Lio! she thought desperately. I want you so much!

'Ready to leave?' Vittore asked gently, when they'd exhausted their goodbyes and her cheek tingled with hearty kisses.

'Uh,' was all she could manage.

'Something wrong?' he asked, his voice unfairly tender.

'I—I…' What could she say?

'Goodbye, my dear.' Honesty hugged Verity hard, then kissed her cheeks fondly. 'What a shame you're not my daughter,' she said, tears welling up in her eyes. 'You're…oh, Verity,' she sniffed, 'I bless the day you came into our lives!'

Released, Verity felt a huge lump of emotion sitting in her throat. 'I've never been hugged and kissed so much in my entire life,' she choked.

'I'm sure that your mother—' began Vittore.

'No.' She drew in a deep breath. 'My adoptive mother favoured Linda. I assumed it was because she was prettier and I was fat and ugly. Looking back, I can't ever recall being played with or kissed goodnight.'

'It's a wonder you're so sane,' growled Vittore angrily.

'Am I? I wonder, sometimes.'

He smiled beguilingly at her. 'Verity, why don't we leave and—'

'Oh, Vittore!' came Bianca's unmistakable silken tones. 'We've only just arrived and you're leaving!'

'My darling!' Vittore's arms rapidly rearranged themselves around Bianca and then her friend, a tall and slender blonde with a shy smile. 'Come around tomorrow and tell me what we've missed. And keep an eye on Mother. I fear she'll dance or talk everyone under the table.'

'I will!' laughed Bianca, her dove soft eyes twinkling with amusement. *'Andiamo, Sofia!'* And she whirled her friend into a fast and furious salsa.

Vittore watched the two women, transfixed. And so did

Verity. Bianca looked wonderful, her voluptuous body infinitely supple, full skirts swishing seductively around her long legs as she dipped and swayed.

Mournfully Verity eyed her own cheap dress and knew she couldn't compete with a goddess in hand-made silk that fitted like a second skin. So she began to push Lio up the hill, quite annoyed with herself for feeling so depressed.

'Sorry,' Vittore said, catching her up a moment or two later. 'I didn't realise you'd gone.'

No, she thought gloomily. What man would?

And it irritated her that she felt so sulky. *Why* was she so muddled about Vittore? OK, he was Mr Nice Guy. Perhaps even Mr Wonderful, if the entire village was right. But she wanted a nice, homely, steady man who had a fixed routine and a nine to five job…

No. She didn't. What rubbish. She wanted Vittore. Wanted him more than ever. It was the vodka loosening her mind, of course. She couldn't even steer a steady course with the buggy. Vittore was having to help her.

'Will you be all right?' he enquired, when she'd eventually popped Lio back into his cot again. 'I noticed you seemed a bit low back there. And you're not too steady.'

Feeling forlorn, she meant to nod but found that she was shaking her head instead. And that tears were trickling down her cheeks.

'What is it?' Vittore asked softly.

'I don't know what's happening to me,' she mumbled. 'I'm so confused.'

'Me too.'

Her head jerked up. 'You?' she sniffed crossly. 'You know *exactly* what you're doing—'

He drew her out to the landing. His hands reached out. Stroked her arms. She steeled her mind to her reaction.

'I wish I did. But every time I come near you,' he said huskily, 'I want to make love to you.'

'You can't,' she said, unable to stop herself from sounding grumpy.

'I will when you're ready.'

His touch was driving her mad. She shuddered and she was in his arms, her mouth beneath his in a breathless kiss that shattered all her good intentions and left her gasping for more.

'Please don't!' she begged dizzily. 'Leave me alone!'

'I can't. If only I could!' he growled, the words thick with wanting and accelerating her own hunger to an unbearable level.

She trembled, moaning beneath the onslaught of his mouth where it roamed the creamy length of her throat.

'I won't let you!' she breathed, gasping when he touched the hollow at the base of her throat with the tip of his tongue.

And then he kissed her so hard and thoroughly that she felt she might faint, her head whirling with an intoxicating excitement that obliterated all sense, all conscience and flung her deep into the darkness of her secret needs.

She felt herself being lifted, the pressure of his chest against her breast, the frantic beat of his heart. Or was it hers? Her head fell back in hopeless defeat and his lips savaged her slender throat with a tender passion that made her cry out in despair.

'Admit what you feel. Drown in pleasure with me!' he growled, gently biting her lower lip.

The softness of a bed met her spine and then his weight lay across her. She closed her eyes, wanting him but afraid of surrender.

'I'll get pregnant!' she moaned, trying to stop him. 'Don't—'

'Hush,' he soothed raspingly.

His hand released the few remaining strands of her hair that were still fastened on the top of her head. She felt his tantalisingly delicate caress as his fingers slid up the nape of her neck. Welcomed the pressure of his body, quivering in anticipation of his touch.

'You're a brute. Dishonourable!' she jerked out in desperation.

'No. I'll prove that. I only want to give you pleasure,' he whispered, sliding down the straps of her dress.

Her back arched as his mouth enclosed her breast. 'Please, Vittore! Don't take me against my will—!'

'I won't,' he murmured, his mouth vibrating against her warm softness. 'But let me show you what pleasure can be yours.'

'What—?' Her voice gave out.

'You will not be harmed,' he said thickly, his hectic kisses consuming her mouth again.

She felt her eyelids growing heavy. Her entire body had been drugged by the richness of his voice, the beauty of his body and the magic of his persuasive fingers.

'Don't...use me,' she said in a tiny, frightened voice.

'Verity!' he whispered brokenly. 'Trust me.'

He touched her then and she knew nothing else, other than pure sensation. With far too great a skill, his hands trailed over her burning flesh, caressing, arousing and sating her need for every inch to be explored.

Fireworks exploded somewhere in the village and with them vanished her reserve. Eagerly she helped him to remove her dress. At some time he must have stripped off his shirt because they were flesh to flesh and she was writhing in fraught delight.

Then it began. A rhythm that dominated her entire self. The intimacy didn't even shock her. Explosions of pleasure flew in all directions as her nerves began to sing. There was nothing but the movement of his hand, the caress of his mouth, the murmur of fluid Italian whispering in her ear...

And all the time the most wonderful, satisfying sensation she could ever have imagined. Wilder and wilder grew her cries while Vittore's soothing grew more intense and husky. Then she lost herself in the incredible vibrations which made her feel she was soaring to the highest mountain, floating on rarefied air that made her breathing short and tremulous, her heart beating so loudly that it felt it might burst.

Sometime, she didn't know when, she wandered down from that peak of pleasure and found that she was lying in Vittore's arms and he was kissing her gently. Warmth permeated her body. The physical ache had gone.

Dreamily she touched his face. 'Thank you,' she whispered simply.

He gave an odd little choke. *'Prego.'*

It was like lying in a warm bath. She sighed and stretched languidly. Vittore's breath drew in sharply.

'And...you?' she asked, solemn-faced.

He moved away and picked up his shirt, his face tight and closed. 'No.'

'But...' She licked her lips, wondering how delicately she could put her suggestion. 'Surely I can—?'

'Verity.' Gravel-voiced and avoiding her gaze, he stood up awkwardly and struggled into the shirt. '*Sleep.* Night.'

He was out of the door before she could stir her dazed, lethargic body. Too drowsy to pursue him, she gave a long, satisfied sigh and fell into a deep, dreamless sleep.

Some time in the early hours of the morning, she woke with the sensation that someone was in the room. Peering in the gloom, she made out Vittore's figure, sitting in a chair and apparently watching her.

She sat up in shock, her eyes huge with alarm. 'What do you want?' she cried shakily. 'Is it Lio? Is he...?'

Her throat dried. He continued to stare as though bemused by her. Verity saw that he was still dressed and clearly hadn't gone to bed at all. Something in his manner frightened her.

'Vittore!' she choked, clutching the sheet to her chin. What was he planning? What was being plotted behind those dark, burning eyes, now that he'd given her such pleasure? 'Don't stare at me like that!' she cried, her nerves screaming with tension.

'I have realised,' he said slowly in an emotion-choked voice, 'what I really want.'

She didn't dare ask what that might be. She was incapable of speech anyway. He stood up, his bulk at once threatening as he came to loom over her, his eyes burning feverishly.

His hand tilted her chin so that she was forced to look at him and she quailed at the intensity of his gaze, shrinking back from the shafts of stabbing pain that slid like knives through her vulnerable body.

He had her, she thought miserably. Wherever he wanted her.

Vittore sat on the bed and stroked her face. She saw that he trembled and gave a whimper of fear.

'Don't you know me well enough yet to realise that I won't hurt you?' he said softly. 'Haven't I behaved honourably towards you?'

Verity nodded dumbly.

'I have burned for you from the moment I first saw you,' he said in a low voice. 'I think you felt the same. Tell me something, Verity. Will you be upset to leave Lio here?'

Again she nodded, her face utterly tragic.

'And he would miss you badly.'

A swallow. More nods. A stifled sob, a tear or two and the tremble of her treacherous mouth betrayed her deep distress.

'You could stay.'

She blinked, unsure she'd heard the barely audible whisper. 'Stay?'

It was Vittore's turn to nod.

'As your mistress,' she muttered bitterly, turning away in such misery that the tears ran in silver rivers down her face.

'No.' He took her chin in his hand again and made her

look up. Gently he wiped her wet-lashed eyes and cheeks with a tissue from a box by the side of her bed.

'As Lio's nanny?' she mumbled resentfully. It was out of the question. She'd still end up in Vittore's bed.

Then he kissed her eyes and kissed her mouth so tenderly that she burst into tears again.

'Hush, Verity,' he crooned. 'I want you to listen carefully. I want you to stay...' He licked his lips as though he was finding his next words difficult to articulate. 'To stay...'

He made a huge effort, squaring his shoulders as if preparing for an unpleasant duty.

'As my wife,' he rasped.

CHAPTER ELEVEN

SPASMS of pain tore into her. She was speechless. This was his solution. He wanted Lio—and would even *marry* to ensure that he secured his son's love!

Aghast, she covered her face with her hands. Hadn't he done that before? Didn't he know from past experience that if he married for convenience instead of necessity that he'd create a hell for all of them?

'I want—' he began roughly.

'I know what you want.' Suddenly ice-cold and composed, she met his eyes. 'And you can forget it.'

He looked grim. Tense and hard-jawed as if he was being forced to accept a terrorist as his bride. It appalled her that he was prepared to repeat his mistake. And it also told her the strength of his feelings for Lio.

'I would never marry for anything other than love,' she said harshly. 'The answer is *no*. You don't need to sacrifice yourself anyway. I've already decided that Lio should live here. I will help you all I can to encourage him to love you. I think it's in both our interests that I leave as soon as possible. You've made it very difficult for me to stay.'

'Not marriage, then. But we could be lovers—'

Her hand dismissed his husky whisper contemptuously. 'I want a life of my own,' she said icily. 'Not as your handmaiden and nanny! You know I want to be with Lio—but not at the cost of my life, my self-respect! I want what all women want—a loving husband and my own children. The answer is still no. Don't insult me by pursuing your own relentless agenda! I have rights! I have needs! And now,' she said with intense passion, her violet eyes almost black with determination, 'I will do everything I can to free myself of you and this place so I can get back to England and pick up the threads of my life! Get out of my room, Vittore. You'll have your precious son. I'll make sure of that. Now go. I need my sleep.'

Without a word, he rose and walked out. She sat there, staring into space, desperately unhappy that she'd been offered marriage by the man she loved—and had been forced to turn him down.

She could see how Linda had been tempted by the wonderful lifestyle, and how her sister had assumed that her beauty and Vittore's good looks would ensure a fairy tale marriage.

For a fraction of a second, Verity had actually visualised her wedding day. Had seen herself gazing into Vittore's eyes and had been tempted to accept his proposal. She loved him so much that she'd thought he might grow to love her too. But then reality had set in.

He would resent her. Might even fall in love, really in love, with someone else and he'd be deeply unhappy tied to her. She couldn't do that to him—she loved him too much.

'Oh, drat and botheration!' she growled. 'When am I ever going to get a decent night's sleep in this house?'

Her plans were working. Gritting her teeth, she had explained them to Vittore. At first he'd refused, but when she'd explained coldly that it was the only way for her to be free in the quickest possible time, he'd grudgingly agreed.

And so, in front of Lio, she and Vittore held hands and cuddled and laughed together—ironically just what Vittore had planned himself. But this time she was in control. Well, almost, and whenever Lio was not looking they would separate and an Ice Age would descend between them.

Lio was calling his father 'Papa' often now. He didn't rush for Verity's arms when Vittore came close. Once or twice, father and son had played in the sandpit together while Verity remained a short distance away.

The final breakthrough came when she suggested that a child of Lio's age might be brought in, and that Vittore could play with this child, thus making Lio jealous.

Vittore had selected the English son of one of his friends in Amalfi, a child almost three years old he'd already taken on treats and who greeted him with satisfying enthusiasm.

Verity watched Lio struggling with his longing to be whirled around like an aeroplane too. He looked back at her and she smiled encouragingly, then deliberately transferred her beaming gaze to Vittore and little Max.

She held her breath when Lio toddled over and stood just clear of the squealing 'aeroplane'. Vittore brought Max in to land and hugged him.

'Me!' demanded Lio crossly.

She saw Vittore swallow, ached at the glistening of his eyes when he turned to his son and held out his hands. Her breathing stopped. Lio's blue eyes were enormous with apprehension. And then he held out his hands too and was being swept into the air, squealing with delight as he dipped and swooped in dizzying circles.

Verity wiped the tears from her eyes. Not long now, she thought, love and anguish numbing her body. Soon she'd leave. It would be better for them both if she did. They'd be able to form a deeper relationship with one another.

The aeroplane landed. And Vittore gathered his son into his arms, his dark head buried in Lio's small neck. Father and son. Together at last.

The poignant scene overwhelmed her with emotion. Tears fell so fast that she could hardly see when the three of them scampered off to the small climbing frame.

It must have been hard for Vittore, remembering to cuddle Max as much as Lio, but he managed. And the joy, the sheer shining radiance of Vittore's face, stabbed such sharp, agonising grief in her loving heart that she had to wrap her arms around herself or cry aloud with the pain.

When she joined in the game of chase, Lio's laughter and the sight of his white-blond head eagerly bobbing after Vittore just made her desperate to scoop him up and hold him close. But she didn't. And knew then, really knew, how desperately it must have hurt Vittore when he was estranged from his beloved child.

Over dinner, he was exuberant, talking huskily of his pleasure, his gratitude.

'I'll never forget what you've done,' he said in a choked voice.

'I am very happy for you,' she said tenderly.

He frowned and looked down at his plate, absently pushing strawberries around with his fork.

'Verity,' he started.

'Sorry. I'm bushed. I'm going to bed. Excuse me,' she said quietly. She couldn't stand any more. Her emotions were in rags.

'Of course.' Politely he stood, but still avoided her gaze and for that she was thankful.

One look from those happy eyes, filled with future plans for his son, would have had her in floods of tears.

Listlessly she struggled up to her room. Flung her clothes anyhow on the floor. Gave her teeth a perfunctory scrub and washed her face. What was she wearing make-up for, anyway? The dash of lipstick and mascara were hardly necessary. Vittore didn't care what she looked like—why should she?

Still in her underwear, she was standing in the middle of her room, staring into space when there was a knock on her door.

'Yes?' she answered wearily.

The door opened and before she could protest, Vittore's arms were around her, his lips on hers, the fluid rivers of Italian flowing over her and weakening every bone in her body.

But she managed to go rigid. To push him away. To

glare and say, 'Get out!' in tones so fierce that she startled herself.

'You don't understand—' he croaked.

'Oh, yes I do.' Her teeth clenched. Every muscle was tensed to straining point. And her anger and misery spilled out in a sudden volcanic explosion. 'You've had a happy day and I'm glad for you and Lio!' she raged. 'But you're not topping it off with a celebration in my bed with my body! Leave me *alone*! Find your own woman. Ask Bianca—'

'She's not interested in men!'

'What did you say?' asked Verity in astonishment.

'Oh, hell,' he muttered. 'It's her business. I hadn't intended…' He drew himself up, cold and remote, his expression pinched. 'You made me say that,' he growled. 'I never like to gossip. But now you know. She's in love with Sofia. They're setting up home together. I apologise for disturbing you,' he said with icy politeness. 'I thought…' He turned away and strode to the door. 'Never mind. I won't bother you again. Goodnight.'

The days passed slowly for Verity. To her joy and pain, Lio became confident and assured, secure in his father's devotion and love.

Now it was Vittore who read the bedtime story, who ensured that Lio was warm enough on the cooler days, always well fed and that he knew how to behave.

For several days now, she'd hardly seen Lio at all. This had been her suggestion, to see if he missed her and became upset. Apparently he and his father had been so busy building sandcastles and netting fish and paddling in the warm sea that her absence hadn't been noticed.

That was how it must be. Soon she would leave and Lio must not miss her.

But secretly she followed them, taking photographs. Vittore. Lio. She loved them both so dearly.

Vittore and Lio laughing as they splashed one another

in the paddling pool. Lio holding Vittore's hands and walking up his father's body then somersaulting backwards. The two of them dozing sleepily beneath the peach tree, Lio with an ice-cream moustache, a small dab of chocolate on Vittore's nose where the affectionate Lio had kissed him.

Tender, poignant photographs that needed a steady hand and often didn't get that. Shots of the house. Of Honesty earnest and engrossed, spraying her precious cuttings.

Verity's heart was so full of love and pain that it hurt. But the good news was that the wall of love that surrounded Lio had changed him into a happy, sunny little boy again.

It touched her heart that he shyly welcomed strangers instead of hiding from them, terrified. And so the villagers were able to indulge him at last. She watched from a short distance as Lio was shown special delights.

The baker's new-born kittens. A bird, carved by the carpenter, that flapped its wings and opened its beak when Lio pushed it along, his beatific smile enchanting everyone he showed it to. Starfish and octopus in the fishermen's nets, paper aeroplanes to chase after along the beach, the art of building sandcastles and watching the sea fill the moat he'd dug with his father.

The wonderfully exciting world of a child. These discoveries that Lio made so gleefully would continue. But she wouldn't be there to watch his eyes widen in astonishment and delight.

Time to go. And she'd do it suddenly, disappear without fuss. She couldn't cope with saying long goodbyes. Lio wouldn't understand her tears and he'd be desperately upset if she cried. That was the last thing she wanted.

Vittore would care for his son and nurture him, she was convinced of that. So what use was she?

Halfway through dinner she pleaded a headache. Refusing offers of painkillers and chalk-white with strain, she escaped to her room. Shaking uncontrollably, she began to pack her things.

In the bottom of the wardrobe she came across the stack of papers belonging to Linda, which Vittore had returned to her after extracting all the outstanding bills.

Numbly she went through them, discarding everything until she came to a sealed envelope. She stared at it for a while before opening it. Several small books fell out and she realised they were Linda's diaries.

She hesitated, but knew that if she didn't read them she would never know the full truth of Vittore's marriage. And it would be a part of the puzzle forever unsolved.

Nervous and tentative, she sat cross-legged on the floor, opened the first page and began to read.

Her heart began to thump. Here it was. Damning evidence that Linda had cold-bloodedly snared Vittore by, as she triumphantly put it, 'copying the sweet, innocent, butter-wouldn't-melt act that's always got that wretched Verity covered in admirers'.

Appalled, she read on. The deliberate pregnancy. The threatened abortion. How Vittore remained polite but distant—and ever faithful; too honourable, too dedicated to the marriage to look at another woman.

Verity skipped the accounts of Linda's affairs, sickened by her adoptive sister's excuse that she needed love in any form, shape or size but wouldn't give up her lifestyle for anyone.

The next part of the diary upset her so much that she wasn't aware of any sound until Vittore's voice broke into her concentration and she looked up to see that he was standing, shell-shocked, in the middle of her room.

'Don't you ever knock?' she cried miserably.

'I did. Several times. I was worried about you,' he said hoarsely. And then she realised why he looked so grim. His eyes were on her case. Slowly he scanned the shelves and flat surfaces, devoid of any of her possessions. His face was ashen. 'Did you mean to sneak out like Linda?' he accused.

'I've been reading her diaries. You didn't tell me that

Linda took your mother's jewels as well as her own, and that she cleaned out your joint account,' she said quietly.

His brows daggered together fiercely. 'I don't talk about her.'

'But she had terrible debts!'

He shrugged. 'She could go through money faster than anyone I've ever known.'

'I can believe that. I know what happened. I'm sorry, Vittore,' she said humbly. 'You behaved like a saint.'

'No. I hope I behaved like a gentleman. Just tell me one thing. Why did she run away when she could have demanded half my fortune?'

Verity bit her lip. 'Because she knew she could lay her hands on money and jewels to set herself up in England and she had a very wealthy lover,' she replied quietly. 'She couldn't bear being loathed by everyone in the village and treated with cold politeness by your mother and the staff. She wanted to be loved and never forgave you for not adoring her. More than anything, she wanted to hurt you.'

'But her plans to marry her lover came to nothing.'

'He left her even before she'd moved into the house.'

She stole a glance at his bleak, harrowed face and debated whether to say that Lio had almost certainly been neglected in England, if the accounts of casual lovers and agency baby-sitters and forgotten meals were anything to go by.

She could tell him that Linda's life had spiralled down into a seedy, debt-ridden trawl for material comfort and that his estranged wife had wished that Lio had never been born—and that she'd also wished she *hadn't* run off with Lio, because he was nothing but a millstone around her neck.

But she loved Vittore too much to disclose such painful information. He was happy now. And deserved nothing that would mar his happiness.

She pushed the diaries into her handbag, intending to burn them later. She knew the truth. She could handle it.

Nothing, not even Linda's sad decline, could affect her as much as leaving the two people she loved most in the world.

'Well,' she said brightly, 'that's the lot. I was going to pop in to see you before I finally left—'

'What flight?'

She started at the barked question. 'Whatever I can get.'

'And Lio? Mother?'

'Oh, they'll live without me very well. Give...' Oh, God! Tears! Hastily she scowled and pretended to be checking the contents of her purse. 'Give them both a hug and tell your mother I'll whizz over one day and we'll talk plants non-stop.'

'I'll drive you.' Scowling, he made to go.

'No!' Sitting beside him for the long journey to the airport would be torture. 'I'm taking a taxi.'

'Expensive.'

'But I won't have to chat to the driver,' she pointed out sharply.

He exhaled noisily. 'I see. In that case, I'll get the rest of your money,' he muttered, looking as if he was very tired all of a sudden.

'No. You've overpaid me as it is. I can make my own way in life.'

'You'll want to visit the nursery to see Lio...'

She glanced at him then, wondering why his voice had broken. His eyes glinted with unshed tears and she felt her own filling her up with grief and spilling onto her cheeks in a total betrayal of her cheery attitude.

'You're crying,' he croaked.

'No!' she sniffed.

'You'll miss Lio,' he whispered, his face so tragic that she wanted to hold him and comfort him and...

She frowned. Why was he upset?

''Course.'

'Let me know when you're coming. I'll send you the return ticket to come over here.'

Vittore couldn't bear it. She nodded, unable to speak and he couldn't keep away from her any longer. In two strides he was there with her, sitting on the floor with his arms around her. She sobbed into his shoulder and he stroked her hair in silence.

She must want this independent life, this…loving husband and… He bit his lip hard, grinding his teeth into it angrily. Yes. She'd have children. And she must want these things badly if she was prepared to leave the child she loved and return to England.

'I'll take care of Lio,' he said, trying to hold back the crucifying emotion. 'Send you photos. Progress report. Perhaps a video, tapes of him talking, perhaps even my mother chatting—that would fill a tape or two.'

She didn't laugh. Instead she clung to him as if her heart was breaking.

'Just promise me one thing,' he said, barely managing to speak at all. 'Don't come unannounced. I—I don't want to be here when you arrive.'

Her weeping ceased. Knuckling her eyes and blinking at him with her incredible violet eyes, she mumbled jerkily, 'W-w-why not?'

He looked at her helplessly. How would he live without her? That smile, the laughter they'd shared, her sweetness…

'You know why,' he growled in resentment. 'Because I couldn't bear to see you and not touch you. Because I will hold you in my heart until I die. I have gained my son and lost the only woman I could love. You are my soul, my life, *mi alma, mi vida, amanda mia. Ti desidero tantissimo*—'

'Vittore!' Her shocked face swam into his vision. 'What are you saying?' she gasped.

He frowned, not understanding. 'You know what I feel. I have, I believe, wanted you from the first moment I saw you. It was like being hit by a thunderbolt. That's why I made that outrageous bet, suggesting that you should become my lover if I gained Lio's trust. I was confident then that I could. And that, once we had made love, you would feel the same way about me. You were always on my mind. You and Lio. And then I wove fantasies about the three of us, living here together, and that's when I knew I couldn't live without you.'

'And...you asked me to marry you!' she whispered.

He shrugged and clambered unsteadily to his feet. It was all over now. He'd make a life with his son and remember Verity to the rest of his days.

'You said you'd never marry without love. Can't force people to love you, can you?' he said, trying to sound cheerfully resigned.

'No,' she agreed and if he'd had any hopes that she'd fall into his arms when he revealed his feelings, they were finally dashed. The pain knifed through him, slicing at his heart. 'Just one thing, Vittore,' she said, her voice shaking oddly. 'I'd like to see the garden before I go. Would you mind coming with me? It's dark and I don't want to break my leg before I fly home!'

Hell was spending time with the woman you loved while she dreamed of a future without you. But good manners prevented him from refusing.

'You'll want to see Lio first.'

'No. After.'

'Right.'

Now he knew what it must be like to impersonate a steel rod, he thought, stomping down the stairs at a safe distance from Verity. Sourly he glowered at her. She seemed carefree as if all her troubles were over and she was looking forward to her new life. Without him. Without Lio.

His rigid frame shook with anger. Everything blurred into a red mist. He had no idea where they were heading or where they were but eventually she stopped and sighed at the moonlit sea and the lights of the settlements around the bay.

'Wonderful.' When he made no comment, she touched

his arm, but he dragged it away. Masochism wasn't his game. 'Vittore,' she mused and he hated her for being so happy, 'I know this is very forward and not the kind of thing that a girl like me should say, but...'

To his astonishment, she grinned and slid her arms around his neck, locking her hands firmly together.

'Don't,' he snarled, despairing when his body betrayed him and said '*please*!'.

'But I love you,' she whispered, stars in her eyes. 'I love you so much I think I will burst if you don't kiss me! I tried not to love you because you were obviously going to send me home, but...what can a girl do when confronted by the most handsome, kind, considerate, loving man in the whole of Europe?'

'You said you didn't love me!' he cried in disbelief.

'I said,' she corrected, 'that I wouldn't marry without love. I thought you were proposing a marriage of convenience because you wanted Lio—and he was attached to me at the time.'

He blinked in astonishment. 'I—'

'Is that it?' she reproved, her laughter ringing out into the hushed night. 'And I thought Italians were romantic! Vittore. Let me make it clear. You love me, I love you. Ask me to marry you again.'

'I—' *Maledizione!* Where was his tongue, his brain, his mind? 'Verity!' He couldn't believe it. One man could not be so lucky, so blessed... 'Oh, Verity!' he whispered. 'I love you so much! I can't...do you...?'

'I love you,' she said solemnly. 'So?' she prompted, her eyes sparkling.

'Marry me!' he blurted out in case the dream ended and he found himself alone and despairing again.

'Yes, thank you,' she said demurely. 'Now, can we make a baby?'

His head whirled. *'Mia adorata—!'*

Verity pulled him down to the soft grass. 'Not words,' she said softly. 'Deeds.'

They were beneath the mimosa, with the stars shining brightly in the great black canopy of the sky. And just before she closed her eyes in ecstatic happiness as Vittore began to kiss her with all the tender passion she craved, she saw a shooting star arc across the sky.

'I wish for happiness,' she whispered. 'For all those I love.'

'Unselfish as ever,' he murmured softly in her ear. 'I worship you, Verity. With my body, my heart, my soul.'

EPILOGUE

'NO, OVER there, yes, by the lilies—what *are* those beetles doing there? Lio, pick them off, there's a darling. And—oh, thank you, Isabella, what a sweetie you are, I'm always dropping my glasses. Just keep an eye on Dante, will you? He's going to do himself an injury with that vicious-looking pruning knife and heaven knows if the agapanthus will recover from his enthusiasm. Oh, Verity! How's everything going? Have they put out the flowers I suggested on the table—'

'Yes, Honesty!' Verity laughed, knowing now to interrupt her mother-in-law loudly or forever remain silent. 'Everything's looking wonderful.'

'He doesn't know?' Honesty asked anxiously.

'Hasn't a clue. The young people are hidden in the marquee and are trying hard not to breathe. Lio, *caro*, I think it's time you shooed all the villagers into various corners of the house.'

'Will do.' Lio, incredibly handsome in sky-blue shirt and cream slacks, placed a loving hand on his grandmother's shoulders. 'Now, *nonna*,' he said sternly. 'You must be quiet until Papa arrives. Do you need assistance? A little sticky tape over the mouth, perhaps?' he asked wickedly.

'Dreadful child!' Honesty scolded, her smile belying her words. 'I don't know what young men of eighteen learn nowadays about their elders and betters.'

'That we wouldn't have half as much fun without them,' Lio said, kissing his grandmother fondly. 'Right. All systems go. Come on Issy. Dante! Get your fingers out of that soil for once. You're as bad as *nonna*.'

Verity felt her heart flutter as her children raced to the

house. Lio, blond, assured, god-like. Isabella, tall and willowy and surely the most beautiful sixteen-year-old on the Amalfi coast. Dante, fifteen, dark and strong and so passionate about gardens that he often worked at night with his doting grandmother and had actually helped Verity on one or two of her acclaimed landscape designs in the area.

A bell rang. The signal that Vittore was arriving. As planned, she greeted him and coaxed him onto the terrace, just out of sight of the marquee.

'Good meeting?' she asked, knowing full well it hadn't been.

Vittore frowned. 'All the way to Naples, only to find nobody there!' he complained. 'I waited for an hour. Had lunch, still no sign of everyone. And hopeless trying to contact them on their mobiles. A wasted day! I can't understand it—'

'Never mind. You're home now,' she soothed. 'I'm sure there's a good reason. I thought we'd have a drink and a simple supper,' she said, feigning tiredness. 'Such a busy day,' she sighed.

'Oh.' He looked disappointed. 'Nothing…er…planned?'

She widened her eyes. 'No. Why?'

'Well… Never mind, darling. I know you've been busy. I'll be happy to be with you. Kids around?'

'Somewhere,' she said vaguely, loving him for not minding that there were, apparently, no birthday celebrations for him. And no sign of a present, either!

It had gone on long enough. She picked up the silk scarf that had been lying ready on the table and waved it casually as if shooing mosquitoes.

Vittore frowned and tipped his head to one side. 'I can hear singing.'

'Really?' She clamped her mouth shut, dying to jump up and down and squeal with delight.

'It is!' He rose. Looked across the lawn. His face was a picture. Verity hugged herself. 'Darling…' he croaked.

Her eyes glistened with tears. Slowly, hampered by all

kinds of difficulties, the large contingent made their way towards them. These were some of the deprived, damaged special needs children Vittore had saved from hell. Many were young adults now, their voices strong and sure and filled with love as they sang for the man they adored.

'Turn around, see who else is here,' Verity said, unable to stem her happy tears.

Honesty, Lio, Isabella and Dante held a banner with the legend 'Happy Fiftieth!' upon it. And behind them crowded the villagers, their voices swelling the sweet singing as they poured their hearts into the melody.

'Oh, my darling!' Vittore's dark eyes glistened with unshed tears. He hugged her hard and then kissed her with gentle passion. 'You arranged all this. You flew them in from all over the *world*... I—I can't tell you what this means to me, how happy I am—'

'We all wanted to show you how happy you have made *us*,' she said, dabbing her eyes. 'I hope you're up to this, old man!' she giggled. 'We've planned to celebrate till dawn!'

'Thank you. Thank you,' he whispered. 'And after dawn, I'll prove to you that I'm not an old man at all!'

Verity laughed and hugged him. Then his children flung themselves into his arms and he was surrounded by dozens of people and she didn't see him for a long time.

She stood beneath the mimosa, listening to the wonderful songs being sung to him, music in many languages sung by people from many countries. But all offered with love.

She smiled dreamily and hugged herself—just to make sure it wasn't a dream. Because she was rich. Not because Vittore was a billionaire, but because he had the ability to draw love to him and she had the good fortune to be part of his enchanted circle. The best riches of all, she thought with a smile and quietly walked back through the magical garden to be with the people she loved.

Your opinion is important to us! Please take a few moments to share your thoughts with us about your experiences with Harlequin and Silhouette books. Your comments will be very useful in ensuring that we deliver books you love to read.

Please take a few minutes to complete the questionnaire, then send it to us at the address below.

Send your completed questionnaires to:
Harlequin/Silhouette Reader Survey, P.O. Box 9046, Buffalo, NY 14269-9046

1. As you may know, there are many different lines under the Harlequin and Silhouette brands. Each of the lines is listed below. Please check the box that most represents your reading habit for each line.

Line	Currently read this line	Do not read this line	Not sure if I read this line
Harlequin American Romance	❑	❑	❑
Harlequin Duets	❑	❑	❑
Harlequin Romance	❑	❑	❑
Harlequin Historicals	❑	❑	❑
Harlequin Superromance	❑	❑	❑
Harlequin Intrigue	❑	❑	❑
Harlequin Presents	❑	❑	❑
Harlequin Temptation	❑	❑	❑
Harlequin Blaze	❑	❑	❑
Silhouette Special Edition	❑	❑	❑
Silhouette Romance	❑	❑	❑
Silhouette Intimate Moments	❑	❑	❑
Silhouette Desire	❑	❑	❑

2. Which of the following best describes why you bought *this book?* One answer only, please.

the picture on the cover	❑	the title	❑
the author	❑	the line is one I read often	❑
part of a miniseries	❑	saw an ad in another book	❑
saw an ad in a magazine/newsletter	❑	a friend told me about it	❑
I borrowed/was given this book	❑	other: __________	❑

3. Where did you buy *this book?* One answer only, please.

at Barnes & Noble	❑	at a grocery store	❑
at Waldenbooks	❑	at a drugstore	❑
at Borders	❑	on eHarlequin.com Web site	❑
at another bookstore	❑	from another Web site	❑
at Wal-Mart	❑	Harlequin/Silhouette Reader Service/through the mail	❑
at Target	❑	used books from anywhere	❑
at Kmart	❑	I borrowed/was given this book	❑
at another department store or mass merchandiser	❑		

4. On average, how many Harlequin and Silhouette books do you buy at one time?

I buy ______ books at one time ❑
I rarely buy a book ❑

MRQ403HP-1A

5. How many times per month do you shop for any *Harlequin and/or Silhouette* books?
One answer only, please.

1 or more times a week	❑	a few times per year	❑
1 to 3 times per month	❑	less often than once a year	❑
1 to 2 times every 3 months	❑	never	❑

6. When you think of your ideal heroine, which *one* statement describes her the best?
One answer only, please.

She's a woman who is strong-willed	❑	She's a desirable woman	❑
She's a woman who is needed by others	❑	She's a powerful woman	❑
She's a woman who is taken care of	❑	She's a passionate woman	❑
She's an adventurous woman	❑	She's a sensitive woman	❑

7. The following statements describe types or genres of books that you may be interested in reading. Pick *up to 2 types* of books that you are most interested in.

I like to read about truly romantic relationships ❑
I like to read stories that are sexy romances ❑
I like to read romantic comedies ❑
I like to read a romantic mystery/suspense ❑
I like to read about romantic adventures ❑
I like to read romance stories that involve family ❑
I like to read about a romance in times or places that I have never seen ❑
Other: ______________________________ ❑

The following questions help us to group your answers with those readers who are similar to you. Your answers will remain confidential.

8. Please record your year of birth below.

19 ____

9. What is your marital status?

single ❑ married ❑ common-law ❑ widowed ❑
divorced/separated ❑

10. Do you have children 18 years of age or younger currently living at home?

yes ❑ no ❑

11. Which of the following best describes your employment status?

employed full-time or part-time ❑ homemaker ❑ student ❑
retired ❑ unemployed ❑

12. Do you have access to the Internet from either home or work?

yes ❑ no ❑

13. Have you ever visited eHarlequin.com?
yes ❑ no ❑

14. What state do you live in?

____

15. Are you a member of Harlequin/Silhouette Reader Service?

yes ❑ Account # ______________ no ❑ MRQ403HP-1B